SNAKEBITE

Beryl Wealand

Snakebite

—⚍—

A Novel

An Arkansas River Valley Mystery

**Introducing Dr. Garnet Daniels,
et. al. (and gang)**

**Pairodocs
Russellville, AR**

D
DOC
C

Snakebite
By Beryl Wealand
Copyright 2014 © by P. B. W. Pendergrass

Author's Note
This is a work of fiction. Most of the characters are alter-egos created individually by relatives and friends. All events are fictitious or are used fictitiously.

ISBN 069221285X
ISBN 13: 9780692212851
Library of Congress Control Number: 2014908398
Pairodocs, Dover, AR

Cover design by Sherry Riggs
Cover photograph by Paula B. Pendergrass
Graphic art by Katelynn McAlister

DEDICATION

This book is dedicated to all my alters who made writing this book so much fun.

1

Dr. Garnet Daniels hurried toward the women's restroom desperately squeezing her anal sphincter and hoping she wouldn't meet anyone on the way. Sliding into a stall and seating herself she waited for the diarrhea and gas to pass, flushing frequently as a courtesy to anyone who wandered in.

"*Damn,*" she said to herself, "*I need this semester to be over so I can stay home all summer and shit whenever I need to without other people wondering what's going on in my guts.*"

Garnet had undergone surgery for a carcinoid polyp in December before coming back for the spring semester at Mt. Nebo State. The surgeon had removed about 10 inches of her ileum (last section of small intestine), her appendix and caecum then reattached the ends during a laporascopic procedure. The surgeon was highly skilled, and there had hardly been any pain. But her bowel habits were still not well trained. The stress of teaching, the pots of coffee, and the irregular meals had resulted in several rounds of IBS, and today was one of those days.

She pulled herself together, put on her "everything is just fine" face and walked back to her office to check in skeleton boxes from the last three stragglers from Gross Anatomy. She checked her emails from the on-campus server noting the reminder about required attendance at Saturday's Med School graduation at UAMS in Little Rock (*Oh joy. I'll get a chance to fart on everyone.*) before heading for home.

The 30 minute drive across the Arkansas River to Russellville was usually her time to make the transition between work and home, but today her brain nattered about upcoming events. Grades had to go in tomorrow; graduation was Saturday; the faculty potluck was Friday and she needed to decide what to take; her niece Colleen would be coming in Saturday afternoon from her third year at UofA; she needed to call her little sister about her other nephew's visit in June (*No wonder I have IBS.*).

—⚡—

By Sunday morning, the world was brighter and considerably less cluttered. She had taken enough lo-motile to make it through graduation plus several days. Colleen had shown up long enough to shove the rest of her stuff into her bedroom before heading out with a frat boy from Mt. Nebo State whom she had met at a weekend party at UofA. Mica had brought her coffee in bed and was rustling up brunch in the kitchen. Yes, life was better. *Oops! Got to run to the bathroom!*

The best part of better was that she had the whole summer off for the first time in many years. Med School faculty had 11 month contracts and either taught or did research year round. Garnet had taken a summer leave of absence to give herself time for some R&R. She was used to pushing herself, but she was almost exhausted and dragging butt. She promised herself she would take it easy and enjoy her summer. No research, no home projects, just sunshine and rest (Maybe. Maybe not.).

2

The next week's stress came from a different source. Garnet's husband, Mica Manfreid, was an Economics professor in the School of Business. His recent publications on agricultural economy related to climate changes had attracted some international attention, and he had been invited to Israel to study firsthand how several pioneering cultivation techniques were successful in circumventing the ravages of drought.

Mica was really excited. Although not religious, he was culturally Jewish. He had studied and learned enough Hebrew for his bar mitzva; and still had the tree certificates from his childhood when Jews from his hometown of Chicago had encouraged donations to be used for planting trees in Israel. He secretly tucked the certificates into his luggage just in case he ever got to see HIS trees!

There was always the possibility that a dustup with Muslim militants could escalate and cause the trip to be cancelled. But things had been calm for quite some time now, and everything looked like a go. Mica's biggest worry was his hip replacement.

He knew it would show up at the airport during security screening, but his mind played with the fact that the replacement had been recalled. His particular model sometimes created microscopic filings of cobalt and chromium which in turn could cause inflammation and could even be toxic. His blood work and MRI were clean, but he hadn't had the implant so long as the people who were showing up with problems. So he took it in stride and joked that he'd know he was in trouble when his hip turned blue.

Colleen was in and out. She was cashiering at Walmart in Dardanelle 10:00 pm to 6:00 am so her love-life was suffering big time; however she still managed to find time to snuggle up to her new love, Dan Stapleton (the BMOC). She had a big date with him on the river coming up Saturday, just to please her aunt and uncle, she brought him by Wednesday afternoon.

Dan was used to playing adults. He "yes-maamed" and "no-sirred" them for almost an hour, laughing at Mica's jokes and complimenting Garnet on everything from her taste in furniture to her choice of earrings to go with her faded shorts and tee shirt. He explained that he intended to go pre-med just as soon as he got finished with football. He knew that he had to keep his grades up so he was taking just the basics now, saving the harder chemistry and biology for when he could focus full time. Then he mentioned that he had been approached by a recruiter for UofA. They were going out on the river Saturday to "discuss" his options. He would have to red-shirt a year if he transferred. But considering the doors that playing football for UofA would open, he had to consider it seriously.

When Dan and Colleen left, Mica sighed loudly, "That kid is so full of bullshit, he farts at both ends."

"Yep", she responded. "He's a real piece of work. I checked his transcript when Colleen said she was going out with him. If he's pre-med, then I'm a purple panda! But he is supposed to be pretty good at football. I hope this is just a summer romance. I don't want to think what might happen if they both end up at UofA this fall."

Thursday night they met old friends at Madam Wu's in Russellville for a leisurely dinner. Friday, Mica spent most of the day finishing up details and making phone calls. He could fly to New York on Saturday via Atlanta, then catch El Al for a direct flight to Eilat. He could have flown to New York on Thursday, but he couldn't go to Israel on Friday because El Al didn't fly on the Sabbath. He had to work with a six-hour time difference, and a two-hour layover in Atlanta to plan his itinerary.

Friday night they went out for an early supper than stopped at the grocery for a two-month supply of M&Ms. Garnet often referred to Mica as her big M&M, and he made sure she always had a full supply around the house. When she got lonely for him, a handful of M&Ms usually did the trick. One summer, when he was gone for eight weeks, she gained three pounds. She vowed this time to exercise more (either that or use a vibrator).

When she returned from Little Rock's Hillary and Willary airport early Saturday afternoon, Garnet was beat. Mica was gone, and Colleen was on the river with Dan and his big recruiter. She ate a handful of peanut M&Ms and climbed onto their bed for a well-deserved nap. She was assisted willingly by Fred Astair, her big black and white tuxedo cat. Fred wasn't the smartest pick in the litter, but he was a great lover. And snuggly naps were his specialty.

3

Dan Stapleton parked his Ford Ranger behind the old school house out of sight of the road and walked out to the highway to hitch a ride back into town. In his mind he visualized the path from the river almost two miles away, through the fields and woods, up the creek to where his truck was parked. He went over it in his mind reliving every detail until his responses were automatic just like he used to do before the games. But this was no football game, and his performance this afternoon could very well be the richest play of his life.

Dan stood beside the narrow road and held up his thumb as several cars passed. He walked a little bit in between and kept trying. Folks in these parts were pretty friendly, and he was sure he'd catch a ride soon. An old man in a beat up green Volkswagen bus stopped and opened the door, and Dan climbed in.

"It's a might warm for walkin'," the old man commented. "A fellar could work up a sweat walkin' in to town today."

"Yeah, I reckon it's goin' to be a hot one all right," Dan returned. "I'm on my way into town to meet some guys to go out on the river this afternoon. That water is sure going to feel good."

"There you go, son. You got the right idea! You from around here anywhere?"

"Over by Clarksville. My uncle Fred has a cabin down on the river, so I've been over this way a lot. Name's Dan Stapleton."

The old man nodded his recognition. "I thought I saw a family resemblance. So you're Fred's nephew? Well fancy that. You playin' any football this year?"

Dan hesitated before answering. He didn't want the old man to remember him too well in case anything went wrong. Still, his Daddy had always told him to tell the truth, it was easier to remember than lies. "Yeah, we won our conference this year; came out second in the regional playoffs, but overall it was a pretty good year."

Dan Stapleton was one of the few boys from the area to make it to college on a football scholarship. The towns and the teams were small and poor and didn't get much recognition. But everyone in the country knew Dan Stapleton was special, and the word got around. He could catch anything you could throw him and run like the wind. His high school team's undefeated season and State AAAA championship had earned him some of the recognition he deserved and a full athletic scholarship to Mt Nebo State to boot. Then the conference and playoffs!

Dan was no dummy. He knew he'd never go pro from MNSU, but there was still a chance he might get a bid from UofA. But he'd have to red-shirt a year, and he wasn't sure he could make the grades he'd need to graduate (forget that med school slop). But, he had a backup plan. Something beside football to pad the nest. They all kept saying he could run like the wind. If his plan worked, he'd need the wind to get him up that creek and back to his truck.

Dan thanked the old man for the ride and got out at the courthouse. He checked his watch; 2:00, still plenty of time. He walked to a sno-cone stand and got a cup of ice. Then he called Colleen. "Colleen? Yeah this is Dan. Say, I hate to put you out, especially since I invited you, but could you drive this afternoon? My muffler fell off, and my truck's in the shop. Thought I'd better get it fixed before I head up to Fayetteville next weekend. Ok, great! Why don't you pick me up in front of Daisy Drugs in about an hour then? Fine, see you then. Wear your sexiest suit!"

Dan walked the five blocks back to his summer apartment that he shared with two teammates. He changed into swimming trunks and pulled a pair of jeans over them. He'd need the protection when he went through that patch of briars. He'd like to wear a long sleeve shirt, but better not be too obvious. He wouldn't have time to mess with rolling his sleeves down anyway. Velcro fasteners on the tennie runners. Couldn't afford to get laces caught in the brush. Drivers' license in the truck. Key in the jeans. Time to grab a towel and some shades and hit the road.

After the football season, Dan had decided to work at home this summer as a river guide. There was nothing like regular hard, dirty work to toughen a guy up. He'd already set up a schedule for regular workouts and daily running to strengthen his legs. He'd spent a lot of time on the river visiting his uncle's cabin almost every weekend during the summer since he was a kid. Guiding appealed to him and the tips were good, especially when folks found out who he was, so he took the job and started working weekends before the semester ended.

It was a lot more work than he had anticipated. He had to get up at the crack of dawn to take the fishing parties out, and he had to be sure all the right gear was together. Paying fishermen were not likely to be sympathetic to a guide who forgot to fill the gas cans. Then there were the parties. He had to select the riverbank sites where there was privacy and the farmers wouldn't get bent out shape about the noise and litter in their fields. Then he had to lug in the grills and the coolers ahead of time and come back later to load them back into the boat to take them to the marina. It was a little like babysitting for a bunch of grownups. Dan didn't especially like it, but it had its advantages.

One of the advantages was the girls. When they found out he was a big college football star, they became very friendly. He'd had more offers this summer than he'd had all year at school. There was something about a little summer hanky panky that seemed to appeal to women. The guys would beg for more when he told this stuff in the locker room. It was amazing how often those little bikini tops came undone when there wasn't a drop of water around.

Colleen Stevens was different. She wasn't like the local girls. She'd come from Dallas to go to UofA and spent off-campus time in Russellville with her aunt who taught at the Med School. He'd met her at a frat party up in Fayetteville. She had a way of coming on like an air head, but somehow you knew she was really putting you on, that there was a keen intellect carefully hidden back there. He couldn't help but wonder why she was so afraid to show people her brain. Maybe it had something to do with her aunt. That old lady had quite a reputation in these parts. She was one of the few local women to have earned a Ph.D. She taught at a Med School, had written dozen of books and campaigned for women's rights all over the state. But that wasn't all. According to the locals she was some sort of mind reader. Dan figured it was mostly hocus pocus exaggerated way out of line, but then, Colleen would look at him funny sometimes like she saw something he was thinking, and she'd kind of laugh at him, and he couldn't help but wonder if maybe she didn't "see" things too.

Dan hoped Colleen wouldn't catch any grief over what he was about to do today. They were going to a river party he had arranged for several couples out of Fayetteville. They were big athletic supporters, and Jim Strothers was on a first name basis with the head football coach. He referred to himself as an "auxiliary recruiter" and had hinted he could help Dan make the transfer. Recruiting by team supporters was strictly off limits, although it still went on all the time. Besides, Dan figured Jim was blowing out the side of his head. The guests were all older, and there weren't any unpaired women, so they had suggested he bring a date. He'd just happened to meet Colleen at Walmart, so he'd asked her along to keep him company. They'd talked several times, but this was the first time they'd had an official date. He was counting on that to protect her. When they found out she wasn't in on the scheme, they'd leave her alone (He hoped.).

There were parties, and then there were "parties." Dan had caught on very quickly. He knew the lower section of the river like the back of his hand, and he had carefully screened and selected three riverbank sites that were almost totally private. He had spent extra hours pulling the brush into protective blinds and spraying the poison ivy with weed killer. From the river, you saw ordinary bushy banks, but behind the brush were selected sandbars where people could enjoy the fresh river air, a little booze, a little sex, and their favorite recreational drug.

This afternoon's party had required special attention. He had guided a small group of three men a month ago at the beginning of the season. Although they had asked him to take them to some of the local honky-tonks one night, they were clearly not interested in picking up women. They had asked him lots of questions, too many questions, about how secluded certain areas of the river were and how often law enforcement officers actually checked parties on the bank. Then they started feeling him out on drugs. At first he thought they might be narcs, and he had been extra cautious. Like many a college athlete, he had used and enjoyed marijuana. When he had to sit out with a knee injury, it had eased his mental pain and made him feel in control again. Now he used it very sparingly. He knew the stuff was a "threshold " drug, and he knew if he got caught football was over for good. Not that it always was when you got caught, mind you, but if he were just a red-shirt next year, he wouldn't have the same kind of clout he had at MNSU. So, he had been cagey with the boys. He had shown them one of his select sites and hinted at the kinds of parties he had guided there, but never committed himself.

Finally they had asked him straight out if he had a good river site where they could smoke a little stuff. He had taken them to a small beach and stayed with them at their invitation. They started with beer and sausages then moved on to dessert. Dan had expected pot (There was plenty in the area.), but these men were chilling with Hydrocodone. They offered Dan a sample. This was really good stuff! He listened as they planned a bigger party with some of their UofA friends, and Dan understood that they weren't just talking. These guys had connections in Northwest Arkansas. They could get anything they wanted from the pharmacy with bootleg prescriptions. One of the guys would bring the best stuff in a prescription bottle. They'd simply put it in one of the coolers, and no one would be any the wiser.

They booked another trip for next week through Dan's boss, with the understanding that Dan would be their guide, then went back to Fayetteville. They had offered Dan a private booking, but he hadn't gone for it. Better to play dumb as long as he could, just in case. At first Dan was disgusted that he had been sucked into the deal. They had sure pegged him right! They knew he'd keep his mouth shut, and he knew there'd be a big tip in it for him. All he had to do was smile and do his job. If the party went well, there'd be other parties, and they wouldn't quit when he went back to school. On the other hand, these guys would know the river pretty well and be able to operate without him, and the gravy would run out. So why not get some of it for himself now?

It was the idea of easy money that had got Dan to thinking. These guys were planning to buy a shit load of street drugs. They must really be loaded. He could buy a lot of the good life at the university for the cost of one party, and these guys would hardly miss it. But what would he do if he had it? No problem. He had plenty of contacts. He wouldn't get the full value, of course, but he could do all right with that. He hadn't had any trouble getting weed last semester, and he knew a couple of team mates who claimed they could get stronger stuff. Or, he could keep it for private parties with just a few of the right people. What would the Fayetteville boys do when they found out he'd scalped them? Nothing. Oh, they'd follow him around and harass him, but these weren't leg breakers or killers. He'd seen killers on the football field, and these weren't killers. They were just poor little rich boys who had more money than they had sense. They'd pay off their dealer just to keep him off their backs and keep their supply coming. Then they'd try to get it out of his hide. But Dan could bluff too. They'd never take it to a court of law which is where he'd threaten to go. He'd claim that he had taken their drugs to use as evidence. He might even turn a small amount over to the Law. With what he had left, he should have a very fine year come fall.

Dan locked the door and slipped the key under the post. Then he jogged back to the center of town testing his knee against the spandex wrapping. It felt good. He was ready. He sat at the counter at Be Well Drugs and ordered two cheeseburgers with everything and a double order of fries. He always ate something before a big game. He was just finishing his chocolate shake when Colleen drove up. He recognized the car from her description on the phone. She'd just got it about a month ago. It was a Mustang convertible that had been painted baby blue. He paid at the register and walked out to meet her.

4

"Hi there," Colleen bubbled up at Dan. "Like it? Isn't it the neatest thing you ever saw? I didn't think Mom was going to let me have it. It's an early graduation present so I'll have it for interviews next year. And I got it painted for free."

He walked around the car and ran his hand over the fenders, checking it out before commenting, "This a beauty, Colleen. And with that color, everyone will know it's you for sure." (*After all, how many baby blue convertibles are there around here anyway*?)

"Yeah, I know," she chirped. "The color was my idea," she beamed. "I've wanted a blue convertible since I was a little girl. Mom said when I was four years old I told everbody I couldn't wait to get my drivers license and my own blue car."

"Yeah, yeah, that's a good one, Colleen," he muttered. He could swear she had air for brains.

They drove out to Bledsoe's River Dock where his trips originated. The Fayetteville party was waiting eagerly. It was getting really hot, and they'd swim and enjoy the water before he fixed up the grills. Jim, the big guy with the beard who looked like an older version of the lead singer for Alabama asked Dan to draw a map for Chet who would be coming later with reinforcements on the beer. Dan figured Chet must be the delivery boy for the drugs. He drew the best map he could. He sure wanted ole Chet to make it to the right spot. No use giving all that good stuff to another party on the river. Chances were they'd make use of the map again later. By then he'd be long gone from the picture.

There were four men and four women. They all looked to be somewhere in their forties. They had that polished preppy look that said they were very comfortable financially with a lot of disposable income. The women were still thin with up-to-date hairdos, unlike the bouffant cowgirl styles you still saw around here, and the men were tanned and well groomed, although tending to thinning hair and a little pauchiness. Dan introduced himself and Colleen, making a point to let them know he was on extra good behavior because this was their first date. He put the couples all in the party barge with Jim at the motor then loaded the party supplies, Colleen, and himself into the second boat and started down the river.

The gravel bar he had picked for today was almost a half-hour down river from the dock. The muted roar of the outboards lulled the passengers who began to relax and enjoy the sparkling current and graveled banks of the winding river. Dan slowed down several times and led them in closer to the banks where he pointed to squirrels' nests and large lazy moccasins sunning themselves on branches over-hanging the banks. Finally they pulled into the bank and crawled out of the boats onto a secluded sandbar. Although they had come maybe ten river miles, they were only about five miles from town and just two miles from where Dan had parked his truck.

They all swam for awhile, and Dan fooled around with Colleen, trying to untie her swimsuit top under water. She was fast as a fish diving down and around behind him to pinch his butt for his orneriness. The women decided they'd like to lie in the sun, so Dan took the men on down the river fishing, leaving Colleen to entertain herself.

"What do you do for amusement around here?" one of the women, Edith, asked leadingly.

"Oh, I guess it must seem awfully quiet to you," Colleen sympathized. "I never noticed it 'til I went away to college. After that it always seemed kind of dead when I came back. It was really kind of culture shock when I first came here from Dallas. Nope, no Cowboys games here! But you get used to it, really. And you do most of the things you do in other places. But folks still get together and drink, and play a little cards, and smoke a little pot, and screw around, things like that."

"Oh, I see," Edith continued. "And, you, do you smoke a little pot and screw around?"

Colleen blushed, "Well, no, not very often that is. I'm always afraid I'll get sick or something. Lots of my friends do, but I'm not much for that kind of thing myself."

"Then you wouldn't mind if we four ladies smoked a little something?"

"No, of course not," Colleen shrugged. "Go right ahead. Just don't fall in the river 'cause I don't think I can swim well enough to pull you out."

Edith chuckled at Colleen's sincerity and opened a small cigarette case from inside her makeup bag. She passed cigarettes around to the other three and offered one to Colleen who declined. The four women made a ritual of lighting up in unison then leaning back to enjoy their hits. Colleen recognized the smell of tobacco and marijuana. Since these cigarettes smelled of neither; she guessed it was something a little more exotic.

When the ladies had settled back comfortably with their cigarettes, the silence of the afternoon settled in around them only to be broken by the sound of a boat motor. It was Chet delivering a very small red cooler with the extra "beer". Edith went down to the water and talked to him in hushed tones, and Colleen guessed there was something else besides beer in the cooler.

When he had gone, Edith opened the lid and peered in. She smiled to herself, obviously pleased with the contents. Then she reached in to retrieve a zip lock bag with more of the same kind of cigarettes.

"Party time, girls," she announced in a sugary voice, and they went through the ritual of lighting up in unison once more.

Colleen was burning with curiosity to see the inside of the cooler, but she was afraid Edith might get mad. After all it wasn't her party. She finally decided to try a ruse when the ladies seemed to be pretty well bombed.

"Oh, am I getting thirsty," she complained. "I know I don't need it, but I think I'll have another beer. Anyone else want another one?"

The ladies all muttered their refusals and Colleen sauntered over to the red cooler Chet had brought and lifted the lid. She took a long unhurried look inside the cooler. "That's not the beer, dummy," she said to herself out loud and moved to one of the other coolers which she knew had beer inside. She fumbled with the pull tab then went back and sat down to imprint the contents of the red cooler in her mind. If anyone noticed her mistake no one said anything about it. Colleen sipped her beer and poured most of it out on the gravel when no one was looking. There was no telling what was coming down with this group. Time to stay alert and sober!

5

The whine of the outboard announced the return of the gleeful fishermen. They had caught several really nice bass, and this accomplishment plus their generous intake of beer had put them all in a jovial mood and ready to party. Dan excused himself to clean the fish and put them on ice while the men joked with the women and joined them at their little party. Colleen followed Dan back down to the water. "Dan," she whispered, "They've got drugs."

"Are you sure?" He feigned surprise.

"Yes, those ladies have been smoking designer cigarettes all afternoon and a couple of them are really potted. What are we going to do?"

"Well," he pretended to seriously consider the situation, "I'm not sure there's much we can do but watch out that they don't fall in the river. They don't really seem like they're going to cause any trouble or anything. I don't suppose it hurts anyone for them to smoke a little stuff."

"But that's not all," she insisted. "They've got a big bunch of pills too. I saw them. We could get in a lot of trouble!"

"Now calm down, Colleen. Let me handle this. Where is it?"

"It's in that little red lunch size cooler. Some man brought it to Edith while you were gone. There's a big medicine bottle of pills and some other prescriptions."

"OK," Dan said to himself. *"Now I know where the stuff is stashed. Now all I have to do is snatch it and make my run."*

When Dan and Colleen returned with the fish, the party was well underway. Jim and one of the other men were engaging in a chugging contest with the other two men waiting their turn as challengers.

"If they offer you anything, take it, but don't smoke it," Dan instructed Colleen. "And whatever you do, lose it before you leave here. Understand?"

Dan egged the two men on and encouraged their game by bringing one of the beer coolers over to the table and lining up several beers behind each man's elbow. They wanted to challenge him, sure of their ability to beat a college man at their age, but he begged off using his training as an excuse. When Jim and his rival had had enough, the other two men began, and soon the group was fully absorbed in the newest drinking bout. It was then that Dan made his move.

He carried the other cooler to the table and set up six beers for each man. Then he busied himself with some snacks at another table until he was sure no one was watching. He approached the little red cooler, turned his back, lifted the lid, and immediately reached for the big bottle Colleen had so conveniently described to him. He stuffed it up under his shirt, clamped his arm over it to hide the bulge, and headed for the woods.

"Hey, Dan, where you goin'? We need some more beer." Jim motioned for him to come back.

Dan's heart pounded wildly in his chest. "Got to take a whiz. Be back in a sec," he waved as he hollered back then continued into the brushy cover.

As soon as he was out of sight of the camp, Dan began to run. He jogged across a marshy slough and up a steep bank to a plowed field of corn. He picked a row and ran straight down it toward the end of the field. He had to hurry to get out of the open in case somebody was following him. He guessed he had plenty of time, but he wasn't taking any chances. At the end of the field, the fence row was grown over in florabunda roses making an almost impenetrable barrier. He searched hurriedly for his red flag then pulled a pile of brush out of the way revealing a narrow tunnel through the briars. He crawled through on his hands and knees thankful for the protection of his Levis.

Dan looked back through the hole furtively. No sign of them yet. Still, all they had to do was follow his footprints across the field. There was no reason to assume they were stupid just because they were drunk. He sloshed across a muddy river inlet to save time, being careful not to get his feet caught in the roots and tangled vegetation. He was just reaching for an overhanging limb to help him climb up the bank when he felt a sharp sting on his right ankle. He kicked instinctively and felt something wriggling under his foot. As he looked, his eyes widened in horror as he recognized the tell-tale square jaw of the treacherous cottonmouth snake.

Normally, he would have killed the snake, but today he was in a hurry. He rushed up the bank out into the pasture where he knelt to survey damage. His heart sank as he raised his pant leg to expose the two bloody knife-like slits. The old boy got him good. The best thing you could do was to be calm and still with a snakebite, but he was a good mile and a quarter from his truck with a pack of angry men on his tail. When he had planned to make a run for it, he hadn't known he'd be running for his life!

—⟋⟍—

Dan had to think fast. He could go for his truck and try to drive himself to the hospital, or he would go to that farmhouse he'd spotted up the hill a little ways. He flipped a coin and called it. He'd go for the farmhouse. There was a little creek that ran down to the river between the farmhouse and where he'd parked his truck. He struck out and picked it up hugging the opposite bank and ducking into the brush. He thought he could hear the sounds of men shouting as the angry foursome followed him from the river. If he could just make it out safely!

Dan left the creek and started up the hill toward the back of the barn. The rapid pumping of his heart was pushing the snake's venom through his body, and he was weakening at an alarming rate. The exertion of the hill was too much for him, and he rolled into the tall weeds crawling forward in a zig-zag pattern on his hands and knees. There was a small pond just below the barn, and it was there that he discovered the nest. An old broody hen had hidden her nest away from the farmer here in the weeds below the pond. She couldn't have gone far since the eggs were still warm.

An idea formed miraculously in Dan's mind. No one would ever find the bottle here, and the hen would never notice an extra large egg. He could come back for his "nest egg" later, that is if he made it to the house in time. He shoved the bottle into the nest and looked up at the back of the barn to get his bearings, noting that the rooster weathervane was in full view from this angle, and plunged on through the grass.

When he reached the barn, he pulled a piece of old board from the side to use for a crutch. He staggered widely as he lurched his way through the pear orchard and to the wire gate at the back fence. A little white dog barked at him madly as he fumbled with the latch. Black and white spots were swimming before his eyes, and he thought he'd never been so simultaneously hot as fire and cold as ice in all his life. A little wrinkled lady came to the door and yelled at the dog.

"Is there something I can help you with, young man?" she inquired cautiously.

"**Snakebite! Snakebite**!" Dan tried to shout, but could barely whisper as he clung for dear life to the fence post then crashed head long through the unlatched gate onto the concrete sidewalk.

6

Colleen had no idea where Dan was going. She saw him dip into the red lunch cooler and guessed he had heisted some drugs, but had no idea what he had taken or where he had disappeared to.

It took a little time before the other guys realized he wasn't coming back. "Where'd that little bastard crawl off to?" Jim asked in a slurred voice. "Hell I could shit twice for the time it's taking him." He staggered off in the direction Dan had taken, and the other three followed. Colleen heard brush crashing and shouting and cursing before the inebriated, drug addled posse staggered back onto the sand bar.

"OK, Missy, where'd he go?" Jim demanded of a frightened Colleen who realized she'd been abandoned with a gang of drunken, drugged, soon to be angry men (The women were too wasted to matter.).

She held up her hands, palms out, in front of her face to signal her innocence. "I don't know," she stammered. "I can't believe he just ran off and left me. How am I going to get home?"

The question stumped the addled man. "I don't know how any of us are going to get home. I don't even know where we are."

"I know where we are," Colleen mostly lied. "We can all go back to the big dock on the party barge. Dan took the key to the Tracker, so we'll have to leave most of your stuff here, but I'm sure someone can come back for it. We'd better go now. It'll be getting dark by the time we get back."

"Yeah, yeah, yeah," Jim eyes were noticeably unfocused. "But first I got to go pee." He swayed his way about three yards toward the bushes before shooting a stream straight up into the air The other three followed suit, dropping their trunks half way down their hips and aiming for an empty beer can. The man called John hit it and announced that he had won the prize. Colleen prayed that they'd pull their trunks up before they turned around.

It took what seemed like forever to Colleen for them to get loaded onto the barge. After several false starts and many exchanges of "Bitch" and "Prick" the group gathered enough of their stuff to satisfy them. They were so wasted they almost left the red cooler, but managed to drag it onto the barge. They left the other coolers, the grills, food and other supplies.

"I'll be happy to drive if you're not feeling so good," Colleen volunteered.

"Now listen here, Missy," Jim retorted. "I am never not good enough to drive a fucking party barge. Just give me the keys. Who has the keys?"

After several minutes of turning out pockets and looking through their dry clothes, John found it in his right sneaker. He was standing on the bank ready to cast off. "I've got it! I've got it! I've got it!" He yelled like a small child. "Here Jim. Start her up." He tossed the key to Jim who was trying to balance himself by hanging onto the wheel. To Colleen's horror, the key went flying past Jim and out into the river.

"God damn son of a bitch!" Jim cursed wildly. "Get your ass out here and find those fucking keys before we run off and leave you."

John worked his way around the side of the boat and dived under water. Soon he came up sputtering. Colleen could hardly believe that she was actually glad to see him.

"Can't see them," he sniveled. "I need some help."

The other two jumped in while Jim held on to the wheel precariously. Soon the three of them had the bottom so stirred up and muddy that even a sober person would have trouble finding the key. The women perked up long enough to hurl insults at the trio, but soon lost interest.

Colleen was busy deep breathing to try to hold down the panic. What now? Then she remembered her cell phone which she had turned off during the party. If she just had some bars, she could call for help. The river gods were with her as she dialed 911 with trembling hands.

"What is your emergency?" the Pope County dispatcher asked.

"Please help us," Colleen heard her own almost hysterical voice respond. "We're stranded on the river, and it's going to get dark!" Then she tried to stay calm long enough to answer the dispatcher's questions: Do you know where you are? How many of you are there? Do you need gas? Are there any medical problems? Colleen had to lie about that. Finally the dispatcher told her to leave her phone on so she could be located with GPS in case it was dark when the rescue team arrived. She also told her to turn on a flashlight as soon as it got dark to help the team find her.

Then the long wait began. Most of the group dozed off until the mosquitoes began to bite as dark approached. No one had thought to bring protection. One woman had a little bottle of Skin So Soft in her bag; she proceeded to dump all of it over herself and the surrounding boat seat before going back to sleep. The others suddenly found it quite attractive to sit next to her and huddled into a shapeless pile with much cursing and whining.

Colleen sat alone back on the sand bar. She had half a mind to untie the boat and let the whole miserable lot float down river. She covered her legs with sand and put on a long-sleeved shirt someone had abandoned. Then she turned on the flashlight she had found in the barge's little tool box and swatted mosquitoes holding back the tears as they all waited.

The sound of a motors coming from upstream roused the motley group. Some of the euphoria had worn off, and they stood (or almost stood) and cheered. Colleen began waving the flashlight excitedly, directing the two big boats toward the cove. Logan, who worked at the marina, had a spare key for the party barge. In short time they were loaded up and on their way to light and safety.

7

Garnet was just waking from her nap when the first call came in. It was Mica letting her know he had made it to New York without too much delay at Atlanta. His brother Sol was there too. Sol had come in from Detroit an hour ahead of Mica, and they had taken a cab to their hotel. They were just getting ready to go out for a nice dinner. They'd leave early in the morning to catch their flight.

"You guys have a great time," Garnet said. Mica and his brother didn't see each other often, and this trip to Israel together was a real treat for both of them. Mica would spend most of his time in academic pursuits while Sol toured the country for two weeks before heading back to the States alone. It was the first visit for both brothers, and they were really excited.

"We plan to," Mica returned. "I'll catch you later in the week. Meanwhile don't eat too many M&Ms," he teased, knowing her tendency to associate chocolate and sex.

The second call about ten minutes later was Garnet's sister. "Hey, Garnet, how ya doin'? Did you get rid of that husband of yours yet?"

"Sure did," Garnet replied. "Where are you?"

"I'm in Cincinnati at an oil conference. You need to come up here; there are some good lookin' cowboys up here this time."

Garnet laughed, "I just got rid of one man. I'm not quite ready for another one yet. I can't believe you're already back in Cincy. Didn't you just move from there to Dallas?"

"Yeah, yeah. But you know me. When I catch the scent of oil money, I'm on my way." Rae owned her own small oil & gas business and was trying to decide where to explore for gas next. "I just got a lease on a hunk of the Fayetteville Shale, so I'll be headin' your way in a few days. Wait 'til you see what I'm drivin'."

"Well whatever it is, I bet it's red. Colleen really loves that little baby blue rig you got her. She's not here now. She went out with one of the football stars from Nebo. Want me to have her call when she gets in?"

"Well la-dee-da! Nah, I'll see her soon enough, and there's no tellin' when she'll drag in if I know that girl. Don't you wait up for her."

The third call was from Colleen. "Aunt Garnet, can you come get me? Dan just disappeared! And the Sheriff's here and the rescue team, and..," the words tumbled out.

Garnet took a quick breath as warning bells clanged loudly in her head: disappeared, Sheriff, rescue team? "Are you all right? Where are you?"

"I'm at Bledsoe's River Dock at London. The Sheriff still hasn't talked to everybody. He said he'd bring me home when he's finished, but it could be a while, and..."

"It's all right, just stay as calm as you can," Garnet soothed in her best take charge voice. "I'll be there as soon as I can. It'll probably take me 20 or so minutes. You hang tight."

—⟋⟋—

Garnet put on fresh clothes and headed out the door, not worrying about her hair or makeup. Disappeared? What in the world? Did he drown? Her stomach was already hurting a little. She began breathing slowly to try to calm herself.

When she got to Bledsoe's, all the lights in the tiny marina were on. Three bedraggled couples sat at a picnic table waiting for the Sheriff to finish interviewing another man and woman. Colleen was inside the little canteen with Harold Bledsoe who had a sober look on his face.

"I'm Garnet Daniels, Colleen's aunt," she said as she offered him her hand. She had found that an honest hand shake allayed some of the discomfort many local men found when dealing with a highly educated woman. No use pretending. They'd find out soon enough anyway.

"Harold Bledsoe," he returned. "Those folks out there were plumb lucky your niece was along. Not a one of them could find their way out of a paper bag. They're lucky they didn't all fall in and drown!"

"Drown," she repeated. "Is, did...?" she couldn't find the right words to ask if Dan had drowned.

"No, no," he assured her. "We're pretty sure he's not in the river, but I'll be damned if I know where he is. He left that sorry gang out there to fend for themselves. And he left a bass boat and about $600.00 worth of my equipment on a sand-bar somewhere! Fortunately I had an extra key so Logan could bring the party barge back. We can't do a blamed thing 'til tomorra morning."

Colleen interrupted, "I've already talked to the Sheriff; he wants to see me first thing tomorrow morning. He said I could go on home now. Please, Aunt Garnet?"

Garnet sensed a quiet pleading in Colleen's tone. "OK, kid, let's get you out of here. You can tell me all about it later. Mr. Bledsoe, it's good to meet you. Thank you for taking good care of her." Garnet talked to Sheriff McCurly long enough to confirm tomorrow's early meeting. It would be Sunday, and she wanted to be sure the Sheriff planned to miss church. Then she and Colleen walked out to the car and headed back toward Russellville.

As soon as they were away from the river, Garnet stopped the car. She unhooked her seatbelt and reached for her niece. Colleen began crying in earnest while the day's ugliness slipped through her tears. Garnet held her closer and rocked gently as Colleen told her what had happened. "Oh, Aunt Garnet," Colleen sobbed. "I was so scared."

8

Garnet didn't get much sleep that night, waking for frequent trips to the bathroom. Colleen got even less rest as the day's events played over and over in her head leaving her thoroughly confused. The next morning neither woman looked up to par. They put brave faces on it anyway and headed for the Sheriff's office.

The Pope County Sheriff, Curly McCurly, was waiting. Garnet had known Curly when his hair really was black and curly. Now it was mixed gray and buzzed. Still the childhood moniker had stuck with him.

When they were seated in a small room with a table and four chairs, Colleen burst out, "Have you found Dan"?

"Yes we have. It took us a while, but when our BOLO located his truck about two miles from where you were on the river, we did some back searching through the 911 logs. We found an emergency call for an ambulance to transport someone with a snakebite from the Staley's not more than a quarter mile from the truck. It seems Mr. Singleton is in

St. Mary's with very serious complications from a nasty snakebite."

"Snakebite? Ugh," Colleen muttered.

"Based on what you told us last night, we went out with our GPS system and made a reasonable trace of his path yesterday. You have any idea what he was up to? They said he was babbling about a nest egg when he came in to emergency."

"Yes and no," Colleen offered. "I saw him reach down into the red cooler just before he left. But I'm not sure what he took. Their whole stash was in there. I didn't recognize any of it. I know the women were smoking some kind of cigarette, but it wasn't marijuana." She glanced furtively at Aunt Garnet to measure her reaction. "There were several little prescription bottles with pills in them, and there were a lot of white pills in a big prescription bottle about the size of baby food jar."

"Hmm," Sheriff McCurly responded. "We searched all of the passengers and the boat very thoroughly. There were three small prescription bottles in the red cooler, and they were all prescribed to Jim Strothers. We called the pharmacy this morning, and they're legitimate. Didn't find anything that big on any of them, and there weren't any drugs on Singleton when they admitted him to the hospital. We made a pretty thorough search along his path, but we didn't find anything there. I wonder where he stashed it."

"Do you mind if we go out and look around?" Garnet asked. "I know the Staleys from 4H when I was a kid. Maybe a fresh pair of eyes would help."

"Be my guest. Another pair of eyes can't hurt, but whatever you do, watch out for snakes."

Garnet and Colleen went out to I-Hop for breakfast then went home to change clothes before heading out to the Staleys. Garnet chatted a while with Mrs. Staley and told her they needed to look for something Dan must have dropped yesterday. They turned down lemonade and walked out past the old barn to the pasture. The orange stakes from the Sheriff's search were still in place marking the presumed path. But Garnet had another idea.

If Dan had hid something as big as a pharmacy bottle, it had to be away from the path. "Look," she said to Colleen, "we're pretty sure he ditched it before he got to the house. He was saying something about a nest egg when he got to the hospital. So what's your best guess?"

"Well," Colleen wrinkled her nose in concentration, "maybe he hid it in something that looked like a nest, a swirl of grass or something."

"Or," Garnet continued, "maybe he really hid it in a nest. When I was a kid, we always had at least one old hen that hid her nest out in the pasture. Let's look around and see what we can find."

They started at the marked path, turned in opposite directions and went out about 20 yards searching for the bottle. Then they both took a step down the hill and worked back to the center, repeating the pattern as they gradually moved down toward the bottom.

"Here it is," Garnet called. "I found it." She waited as Colleen made her way toward her. They separated the tall grass carefully to expose the broody hen's nest. There were two broken eggs and a big bunch of feathers. Garnet felt the nest. It was cold. Something had frightened the hen off her eggs. She would not be returning.

Garnet and Colleen searched the area around the nest. They found the toe print of a sneaker, probably Dan Stapleton's, and some broken weeds, but no other evidence of human intrusion.

"It was here," Garnet stated firmly. "All the markers are right. I haven't seen a nest like this in years. Whoever, or whatever, chased that old hen off and broke those eggs also took that bottle! I'd bet even money that a big black snake took it. I remember when I was a kid Mom had me kill a big ole snake because she was afraid it'd eat her baby chicks."

"Now if you were a snake," she asked herself out loud, "where would you go to hide? Why, in the corn crib, of course! Where there are mice and other good rodents to eat. It's almost as good as the chicken coop!"

The Staley's corn crib was empty this time of year. Except for a big barrel of corn for the one old horse, they rarely had occasion to feed corn anymore. One of the neighbors usually brought her a load of scrub stuff late in the fall, but most of that was gone now. It wasn't like when they farmed for a living and they stored enough corn there for the whole winter.

With Colleen close behind, Garnet opened the crib door and quietly climbed the three steps up into the crib. She felt a cobweb across her face and brushed it away with her hand. She turned on the light switch and looked around the boundaries of the room listening as mice scurried for cover. She started to scan the crib again after her eyes adjusted to the dim light of the single naked bulb and smiled when she saw the mouse. It ran from the shadow of the feed barrel and dived through a knot hole in the brittle floor board. Garnet walked softly to the hole and listened. She could just make out the intermittent thumping produced as the snake twisted its body against the joists trying to relieve its agony.

Garnet used a broken hoe and an old piece of single-tree to pry up the boards. Then she looked for movement as she scanned back and forth between the joists, using her ears as much as her eyes. The snake was in there in a corner between the floor joists! "Quick," she instructed Colleen. "Go out to the van and get the flashlight from the tool box. It's too dark in here for me to be snake wrestling."

While Colleen went for the flash light, Garnet retrieved a big tow sack that was hanging on the wall.

Colleen reluctantly held the sack while Garnet fished for the snake. Although it was in no condition to put up a fight, it was still strong enough to make the task of getting it into the bag quite difficult.

Garnet took the sack from Colleen, opened it, and laid it beside the hole in the floor. Then she blocked the escape route with her feet and used the hoe to pen the snake and rake it toward the bag. She used the piece of single-tree to prop the mouth of the bag open then scooped the snake in that direction. The single-tree fell over, and the snake ended up on the bag, but not in it. Colleen made a rapid retreat back down the steps.

Finally, Garnet gathered up all her will power and grabbed the six foot snake just behind its head with her right hand. If it had been healthy, she could never have held it, but it had been weakened with pain, so she was able to manage. She grasped the snake's tail in her left hand and shoved it deep into the bag feeding the body in coil by coil. Finally she released the head and gathered the opening of the bag into her hands capturing the snake inside.

When they had finally secured the sack with a pink woven bracelet from Colleen's wrist, and had begun breathing normally again, Colleen ventured a question. "Aunt Garnet, do you think the snake really has the bottle?"

"We'll see," Garnet let out a big breath. "Now let's get this bad boy home. I have some calls to make."

—⁓—

The first call was to Dr. Jeremy Clayborne, chair of Biology and Fisheries & Wildlife. They'd met at several conferences on the anatomy and physiology curriculum for Biology majors, especially those who were pre-med. Without giving too much information, she asked for the home number of their herpetologist, Dr. Stephanie Gleason, and called her immediately.

Dr. Gleason had just come in from the field where she was collecting fence lizards for a new study. It didn't matter that it was semester break, the work had to be done when the animals were most likely to be available. Garnet explained her problem and they agreed to meet at Dr. Gleason's lab at 5:00 with Garnet bringing the snake and the ice. Meanwhile, Garnet put the bag in the bottom of the refrigerator in the garage to cool the snake down and slow its movements.

Colleen was fascinated by Dr. Gleason's lab. There were snake, lizard and turtle specimens all over, and several aquaria held busy little salamanders. Several fence lizards were sequestered in a large wire cage. What really impressed Colleen was that Dr. Gleason was female. Colleen hated to admit it, but she was prey to the old male-female stereotypes that ruled out a woman's conducting meaningful research in the field.

Dr. Gleason pulled an old-fashioned galvanized tub from under a lab bench. She and Garnet hoisted it up onto a table before filling it with ice. "I'll let you do the honors," Garnet offered. She was sure Stephanie was far superior to her at handling snakes. She had really struggled to get the big guy into that sack.

"OK," Stephanie agreed. "But first let's cool it off. The two of them gingerly lifted the tow sac and settled it on the ice. After about 20 minutes the sack's wiggling slowed noticeably. Then Stephanie unwrapped the pink arm band and slowly opened the sack. "Yep," she said. "He's almost ready. Help me straighten him out to get a more uniform cool down."

When the herpetologist was convinced that the snake was cold enough to be anesthetized, she opened up a leather pouch of dissecting tools, and the two women took a better look. "There they are. See them?" Stephanie asked Colleen who didn't see a thing. "Let's see what we have here." She gently prodded and squeezed two small, and one large lump on the upper third of the snake's massive body. "Looks like maybe two eggs and something really solid. Probably your prescription bottle."

With Stephanie doing the surgery and Garnet assisting, they gently opened just enough of the body cavity to expose the gut. The snake twitched reflexively when Dr. Gleason cut into its body giving both Colleen and Garnet quite a start. Unfortunately they would have to enlarge the opening to get the hard lump out. They left the two presumptive hen's eggs intact; no need to do more cutting than needed.

Stephanie cautiously made an oblique slit in the gut trying to follow the outer muscle plane. The area was bloody and raw inside. Garnet was not at all sure that the snake would recover. Quite possibly the damaged section would burst after the surgery. Stephanie cut through the wall and removed the jar. Then she decided to remove the necrotic section. It was a gamble, but she felt obligated to take it. She cut out the worst of the damage then picked up a quail egg. Garnet held the two ends while Stephanie inserted the egg into the upper end of the intestine and used it as a plug to make sure she didn't sew the gut closed as she connected the two segments. Next she gently forced the egg upward in the tract crushing it in the process. Perhaps the snake would be able to absorb some of the protein while it mended. She sewed up the muscles on the belly, and they lifted the snake and coiled it loosely on the bed of straw in a 50 gallon aquarium. The surgery was finished.

"Look," she pointed to the snake's stump of a tail. "Our boy has been injured before. At least we know he healed up once. Let's keep our fingers crossed for this time."

"How do you know it's a male?" Colleen inquired.

"Oh, it has a hemi-penis," Dr. Gleason explained gently squeezing the snake's genital plate to show the two little worm-like projections. "Definitely a male."

—⁓—

Garnet called Sheriff McCurly on his cell and arranged to meet him at the house. Then she changed gloves, picked up the vial, and put it into a fresh zip type bag. She asked Stephanie for a long piece of tape. After securely sealing the bag with the tape, she signed her name across it and dated it; Dr. Gleason followed suit.

She thanked Stephanie, and they agreed to have lunch together later in the week. By then they could see how the snake was doing, and Garnet hopefully would know more about the bottle.

9

Sheriff McCurly was bushed when he knocked on Garnet's door late Sunday evening. He had missed church with his family to begin collecting information. After plotting Dan's path and looking for evidence, he and two officers had spent most of the day compiling a list of leads to pursue first thing tomorrow morning since most of his personal contacts in the northwest corner of the state wouldn't be in their offices until tomorrow. According to Google, the ID on Jim Strothers was good. The fool obviously had more money than he had sense. He was a well-placed business man in Fayetteville, the owner of a very successful car dealership catering to well-padded local business men and some big athletic supporters (so to speak). There was a good chance he had plenty of expendable income. What bothered the Sheriff was that he couldn't pin down illegal drug possession. He knew the whole group was wasted when they came into the dock, but they'd been out in the sun all day drinking, and Jim had given permission for a search with no hesitation. The pills appeared to be legitimate prescriptions, and without knowing what was in the big bottle, he couldn't make much of a case.

Jim's date, Edith House, had no legal ties to him. He was separated and in the middle of a nasty divorce settlement. Business sources in Fayetteville said he tended to play the field and the lady could be one of several current love interests.

The character, Chet, who had delivered the red cooler was especially worrisome to the Sheriff. He had materialized from nowhere and vanished into thin air. The kid behind the counter at Bledsoe's said a woman had come in to ask for the map Strothers had left. She gave him some story about meeting her brother who was waiting down river. When pressed, no one could describe her very clearly except that she had light brown permmed hair and wore a plaid blouse and denim skirt. The man had been very careful not to be seen either in town or at the gravel bar where he kept his head down and wore a cap pulled down over polarized shades. Edith had taken the cooler from him, but she was no good as a witness. Colleen couldn't give more than a vague description. Chances were even though Strothers and his bunch were pikers, the man in the glasses had been a pro. He had known who and where. If he were local, how did he contact someone from Fayetteville? The sheriff didn't like the idea of pushers on his river, and he was going to do something about it.

Sheriff McCurly kept hoping to get a chance to talk to Dan Stapleton. He had instructed the hospital staff to make a list of family members and keep everybody else out once Dan was out of intensive care. Right now Dan was the only one who had been really hurt. If the sheriff could stop this dope dealing right here, maybe he could keep it that way.

Garnet led him to the large kitchen where she served him a big glass of iced tea at the counter. They didn't waste time on small talk as Garnet opened the refrigerator and pulled out the zipped bag. Sheriff McCurly turned it over in his hands and smiled as he saw the seal with two names signed across it.

"Well, that takes care of one very big chain of custody problem. How did you and Dr....(He squinted at the name.) Gleason know to seal and sign?"

"Oh, that's easy," Garnet explained. "We watch a lot of television. No seriously," she continued. "We handle a lot of confidential student information at Mt. Nebo, and it's standard protocol to seal and sign over the seal. Besides, Dr. Gleason keeps track of her specimens by sealing and dating."

The sheriff studied the label on the bottle intently. "It looks just like the others from the cooler. I had Justin take good pictures so we have something to compare it to. It says Jim Strothers all right. But why would a doctor prescribe 90 Hydrocodone pills? Ah, well, something else to check out tomorrow. It's hard to read the doctor's name; its really smudged, probably from being inside the snake. I'd be thrilled if it had some fingerprints on it, especially Dan Stapleton's. We have a lot of circumstantial evidence against him, but a fingerprint would really be nice."

"I asked Stephanie about that. She said very little digestion had taken place. There were two eggs with it and they were cracked, but not crushed. Poor snake! There's a good chance for finger prints on the ends of the bottle, but probably not on the sides that were rubbed by the lining of the intestine. How long before we get a report?"

"Well," he sighed. "It may take two or three weeks. The State Crime Lab is backed up from that bank robbery two weeks ago. They're not known for their speed, you know."

"Are there any other options?"

"The only other one I know is Hattie West. But I really don't have any discretionary monies left. That house fire back last spring really hit us hard, and we've been to the Quorum Court with our hands out ever since then."

"Let me talk to her. I hear that she's always looking for current data for her classes. Everything is numbered to protect privacy, so the names of the guilty would be protected. I know for a fact she's teaching this summer, because I promised her I'd come in if any human bones showed up."

"That sounds great to me. Meanwhile I'd better take custody of the evidence. There's no tellin' what you'd do with it overnight," he joked. He lifted his weary bones and said good night. Garnet closed the door and ran for the bathroom.

10

Dan Stapleton awakened from his coma screaming in terror. A large cottonmouth was wrapped around his neck and its ugly head was striking straight at his face, fangs bared. As he looked around the room, he was certain he had entered another space in his dream, a space that had no familiarity or meaning. But wait a minute, whose solemn faces were those hovering close, whispering anxiously. He had seen them before, but who were these people?

A nurse came and took his vital signs. Blood pressure still quite low. She spoke to him gently, yet firmly. Did he know who he was? How did he feel? Then she stepped back and motioned to a man and a woman, cautioning them to limit their questions. They leaned over him and called him Son. The woman kept patting his hand and trying to hold back the tears that ran down her face and under the edge of her chin. Where was he? And who were these people?

The next time he awakened, a great deal of the fog had lifted. There was a different nurse in the room, and the man and the crying woman were gone. Dan figured he must be in a hospital some-where, but he wasn't sure why. Had he been in a football accident? No, he didn't think he was play-ing football now. Maybe a car accident then, or had he fallen in the river and drowned?

He cleared his throat, and the nurse looked up and smiled. "Well, hello there," she said pleasantly. "They said you were coming out of it. Let me go find the doctor. There now, how do you feel?"

"About half dead. What happened?"

"Do you remember anything?"

He shook his head and she went on, "You were guiding a river party on the Arkansas and got snake-bit. Bring back any memories?"

Again he shook his head.

"Oh, well, most of it will come back to you, later. Don't worry about it. It's very common for people to lose all memory of events that happened just before a major trauma. OK, here's the doctor. Let's let him look at you. Then we'll see if you feel up to seeing your family."

The doctor checked his corneal reflexes and tested the strength of his grip. He wrote a few com-ments on the chart then signaled the nurse it was all right to bring in the family, but just two of them, and for just five minutes.

This time Dan recognized his parents. His mother was still crying, but she seemed greatly relieved. He found out from them that he'd been in a coma for a little over two days. But everyone kept telling him not to worry. His memory could come back later.

During the next few days Dan learned the grisly details of his accident. He had been guiding a river party on the Arkansas. For some unknown reason he had left the river and had come out on farm land. He had been snakebitten and had made his way to the Staley farm where he had collapsed after asking for help. He must have run for help because the venom appeared to have spread widely throughout his body. His blood pressure had fallen dangerously low, and even with the anti-venom it had been touch and go.

The biggest shock for Dan was when he saw his leg. His ankle was swollen to about three times it's normal size, and his leg was black all the way up to his knee caused by the hemolytic effects of the toxin. There was only one word for the way it looked: Rotten. They had elevated the leg slightly to help keep the swelling down, but not enough to push the toxin toward his heart. He tried to move his toes, but the muscles in his leg seemed to be paralyzed. And the pain! God, the pain was awful. It was worse than his knee surgery had been. And the wracking nausea and low blood pressure left him weak and light headed. Sometimes he had to close his eyes just to keep the room from spinning. They moved him out of ICU to a private room. It would be several days before he would be released to go home to a long convalescence. If his memory didn't come back, he could easily lose a whole term at the University. What if he lost his football scholarship?

After his parents, the next person allowed in to see Dan Stapleton was Sheriff McCurly. The Sheriff asked Dan some questions about the people at his party and about a pharmacy bottle that just might have been stolen. Dan still didn't remember much, but something told him he'd better play dumb anyway. The Sheriff mentioned Colleen Stevens' name. Dan vaguely remembered Colleen having been with him sometime last week. Something about a blue car, but not much else. Maybe it would all come back to him, later.

When it did start coming back to him, Dan decided he'd better talk to Colleen. Nobody else would tell him what the hell was going on. She'd been there. Maybe she'd tell him.

Colleen was thrilled when Dan's folks called from the hospital. Dan wanted to see her. She'd been awfully worried about him. She changed clothes and drove over immediately.

"Hey, Colleen," he greeted her, "how's it going? What you been doing with yourself lately? Been taking anymore river trips?"

"No, not really. I've been really worried about you. Well, it's not just me. Everybody's been worried sick. I guess you're not going to be playing much football this season, huh?"

Dan pulled back his sheets and showed Colleen his blackened toes. "No, not with this much damage."

Colleen cringed at the sight of the rotten-looking toes. "Oh, damn, it's worse than I thought. You've really got it bad! How are you going to survive this?"

"I'll be ok, I guess. Anyway, everyone says I'll be good as new a year from now. A year from now! Can you imagine? By then I'll be out of training. Colleen, I'm never going to play football again." Tears came to his eyes as he admitted out loud what he knew in his heart was true.

"I'm sorry Dan. Is there anything I can do?" She brightened perceptibly. "I can come to see you every day until I go back to school."

He looked crestfallen at the mention of school.

"You are going back to school, aren't you?"

"I don't know yet. I've still got almost two months. The doctor isn't sure how strong I'll be. I seem to be one of those people who's extra sensitive to the venom. I just about killed myself running for help. I pumped that venom all through my body. But I couldn't afford to let Jim and the others catch up with me."

"So you do remember then?"

"Yeah, I remember enough of it to keep my mouth shut. If I can just get out of here; I think I can get back to where I hid the stuff."

"It's not there."

"What do you mean? Did you follow me?"

"Don't be stupid! Of course I didn't. That was your play, and your play alone. And you probably got what you deserved!"

She looked at his shocked face and relented. "I'm sorry. I didn't mean that. I was just mad at you because you kind of set me up."

"Hey, thanks, Colleen," he buttered her up. "You've been more straight with me than anyone else. I shouldn't have set you up, but I was afraid it you knew anything you might get hurt. Those guys could get pretty nasty, you know? I really appreciate the way you covered for me, even if it didn't work out. The truth is... Well, I get awfully lonely lying here all day, and I've been thinking about you a lot. What you said earlier, about coming every day? Did you mean that?"

Colleen nodded shyly and kissed him on the check. She'd be back tomorrow, sure thing.

That night Dan Stapleton couldn't sleep. The pain threshold was rebounding, and the edge of pain was pushing past the drugs. He had experienced this with his knee. In the hospital, and again later when he'd pushed too hard training, the pain had come to stay, throbbing at a deep level, wearing him down and spacing him out. That's when he had turned to marijuana. Just a few hits and he was back on top of the world. He could endure the grinding pain and regain control of his mind and body.

But where could he get marijuana here? Who could he trust to bring it to him? There were no sympathetic team mates or over-enthusiastic supporters. He was out of the limelight in a small town hospital filled with small town minds. But wait. There was one person who just might be able to help. He'd ask Colleen tomorrow.

Dan waited impatiently for Colleen all morning. When she finally arrived at two o'clock, he was over-anxious and irritable. "Well you certainly took your time getting here!" he snapped. "I tell you I'm lonely, and you come waltzing in here like it doesn't matter to you!"

"Well, excu...use me!" she countered sarcastically. "If I'd known you were going to be such good company, I'd have been here at five thirty this morning!"

"I'm sorry," he backed down. "It's not your fault. It's just that I'm so edgy. The Hydro is losing it's effect, and I'm really in pain. It happened when I had my knee surgery too. But then I was able to do something about it, if you know what I mean."

She shook her head blankly. "No, I'm afraid I don't. Should I?"

"You know, marijuana. It takes the edge off and makes the pain bearable just like marijuana does for cancer patients. I really need a joint."

"Oh," she said flatly, "That's too bad. I don't think they're going to give you any here, Dan."

"Of course not!" He gritted his teeth in exasperation. "But you can get it for me."

"Me? You've got to be kidding!"

"No, no, now you calm down. Just calm down," he pleaded. "Look, it doesn't hurt anyone does it? And I'm really hurting, Colleen. Honest. If I weren't, I wouldn't ask you, OK? I just thought maybe you were the kind of girl who'd be a real friend. That's all."

"Well, it doesn't matter anyway," she relented slightly. "I wouldn't know where to get any stuff anyway."

"No, of course you don't. I can tell you're not that kind of girl." He closed his eyes, and the sweat popped out on his forehead as he grimaced with pain. Whatever else about him was fake, the pain was real.

Colleen stood watching silently. Then she spoke firmly. "Ok, I'll get it for you, but you'll have to tell me where."

Dan spoke in short bursts between waves of pain, "Go get my right shoe out of the closet. See the Triple-A card? There's a number written in. That's... a local number," he gasped for air. "Here... in Pope County. Ask for Hot Dog, and tell him... I sent you. Tell him... you want marijuana. Get... three joints... I don't have any cash. Are you good for it? Thanks.... I'll wait for you."

———ᴠᴠ———

Colleen was trembling as she made the call on her cell from the hospital lobby. She'd never done anything like this, and she was scared. What if someone found out? Never mind, she calmed herself. It was just a business deal. That's all. Besides it wasn't for her anyway. And it didn't really hurt anybody. Couldn't they see how much pain he was in?

Hot Dog agreed to meet her at the Dr. Dog (how appropriate) on highway 124. She went by the bank and used her ATM card to get money. She forgot to ask him how much. She hoped three hundred would be enough. Dan had better be good for this!

She sat in her baby blue car and ordered a burger and fries. She was almost finished when a young man in a pair of coveralls approached the car. He wore black glasses, and his hat was pulled down over his face. Colleen wasn't sure, but his brown hair had an artificial look. A bad hair weave maybe?

"Hey, aren't you Dan Stapleton's girl?" he asked her familiarly.

"Well, no that is ---I---" she stammered.

"Name's Malone. Hot Dog Malone," he emphasized the code name. "Used to play basketball with Dan. How's he getting along?"

"He's really sick," she confided earnestly. "I think he'd really like to see you."

"Sorry, can't see him today, but I'd like to send him a little something. OK?" Colleen nodded, still unsure how this was working out.

"Here, give him this for me, will you?" He handed her a small gift wrapped box with a card. "Tell him I couldn't get three today. Maybe tomorrow. But these two goldens are on me. Understand?"

Colleen nodded, and Hot Dog Malone disappeared.

It was during afternoon quiet hours when Colleen reentered the hospital. She didn't want to take a chance on the presence of relatives when she tried to deliver the package, not really sure herself what was in it. She climbed the stairs to the third floor and waited patiently for the nurses to pass before she slipped into Dan's room. The curtain was drawn, but she could hear him moaning as he tossed in his bed.

"Dan?" she whispered. "Are you awake? Look, I got it. Hot Dog said he just had two today, but they're on him. He called them 'goldens'. Maybe more tomorrow. OK? I didn't have to spend any money."

Dan's eyes lit up as he saw the package. Colleen took the paper off slowly so the noise wouldn't carry into the hall. She broke the tape on the sides of the box and opened it to show Dan the two cigarettes lying innocently on the cotton. Dan signaled that he wanted one. Colleen placed it in his lips and fumbled in her purse for a book of matches trying hard to keep quiet.

Dan smoked slowly, taking long draws on the weed and savoring the smoke fully. It would take a few minutes for his lungs to transport the drug to his brain where the effect would be translated. The tension around his jaw eased as the pain ebbed gently away. It was just like he remembered from before. Good-bye pain and despair. Hello peace and control.

Suddenly, Dan's head lolled to the side and his mouth fell open as he tried desperately to get his breath. His chest heaved, and he went into convulsions. He dropped the joint which rolled on the floor and extinguished. It was the marijuana! It was killing him! He was dying right in front of her!

Colleen bolted from the side of the bed and ran to the door where she began screaming hysterically, "Somebody come quick! I've killed him! I've killed him! I know I've killed him!"

Colleen sat huddled in the corner dejectedly. The hospital floor was a furor of activity as the medical staff responded to the code on third floor. People and equipment flew down the hall to Dan's room as the emergency team worked to revive him. They had seen the effects of drug overdose before as patients entered the emergency room with symptoms resembling a heart attack. This time it was worse. The patient was really weakened from the snake bite. And to complicate things, there was the existing medication for pain and nausea which clearly was interacting with the marijuana (Any fool could smell it.). If he pulled through it would be a miracle. Right now the best they could do would be to stabilize him.

One of the hospital security officers removed the gift box and the remaining charred butt from the room and locked them in the downstairs safe. They would need the evidence if the family decided to sue. The head of security came to where Colleen was and escorted her to the Director's office. This young lady had a lot of explaining to do.

But Colleen would not explain. She sensed that she was in deep dog doo, so to speak. Getting caught with marijuana was one thing. Administering a lethal dose was quite another. She stubbornly refused to tell them anything except her name, address and phone number. At first they cajoled. Then they wheedled. Finally they became overbearing and threatening.

"Now look here, young lady," the Director stated firmly, "You're in a lot of trouble, and you had better talk to us. We're going to get to the bottom of this one way or another, so you'd just as well cooperate now as later!"

Colleen held back the tears as she responded equally as firmly, "I know I'm in trouble. And I know you deserve an explanation. But I'm really scared because I don't know what is going to happen here either. I'm not trying to be unreasonable, but I'm not going to talk to anyone until I see a lawyer."

The Director threw up his hands in exasperation. "Ok, have it your way. I have no choice but to call the Sheriff."

Colleen knew that the Sheriff's office had already been called, but she nodded her agreement anyway.

Sheriff McCurly came in person to take her to the Pope County Detention Center where all drug cases in the county were processed. Like the Director, he tried in vain to question Colleen. She asked if she could make a phone call.

"Aunt Garnet, this is Colleen. I'm at the Pope County Detention Center. They're saying I tried to kill Dan Stapelton. Can you come quick? I need a lawyer. I gave him some marijuana, and he went into convulsions. They think he may die. OK. I'll wait. Good bye."

11

Garnet hung up the phone and smashed her fist against the kitchen counter, "Damn! Damn! Damn! Colleen, how could you be so stupid?" (*Marijuana in a hospital! Where does she think this is, Colorado?*)

She picked up the phone book and turned rapidly to the yellow pages for attorneys then jotted down a number. "Judy, this is Garnet Daniels," she spoke to William Turner's receptionist. "Is Bill in? Look, I hate to bother him, but Colleen's in big trouble. She called from the Detention Center. She's in jail. I don't know all of it, but she said she gave Dan Stapleton a hit of marijuana, and he went into convulsions. They could charge her with murder, couldn't they?"

"You'd better come on over here," Judy instructed. "He's with a client, but should be just about finished. I'll make sure he doesn't take off somewhere."

Colleen sat alone on a folding chair in a tiny room at the Sheriff's office. Sheriff McCurly had read her rights, and she had asked for a lawyer. She told him her aunt had been called and was making arrangements. The District Attorney had been in to see her, and she knew there were news reporters outside. She wanted to scream, but instead she repressed all emotion until she felt numb and heavy inside. Was Dan dead? Why wouldn't someone tell her? She wanted to ask, but she was afraid to find out the truth. Better to wait.

It was almost three hours of eternity before Garnet and the lawyer arrived. Colleen had not been charged yet when they arrived. Her refusal to reveal any details had kept them all confused about just what had happened.

William Turner would be present during questioning. Garnet would have to wait in the lobby. According to the Director of the hospital, young Stapleton had pulled through. He was going to be in ICU a couple of days, and there might be some permanent damage to his heart. At least they weren't dealing with murder. Attempted murder, maybe. But not murder.

Encouraged by the presence of a lawyer, Colleen told her story as straight forwardly as she could. She told them how Dan had begged her to help him ease the pain. How she had made the call to the number in his shoe. How she had been contacted by Hot Dog Malone. And how she had delivered and lit the ill-fated joint.

"I didn't mean to hurt him," she pleaded as tears began running slowly down her cheeks. "I didn't know what it would do. I wouldn't have hurt him for anything in the world." Then she looked up at the Sheriff. "Is he...? Is he dead?"

"No," the lawyer reassured her. "No he isn't, and these gentlemen should have told you that. If you were laboring under that impression, then your statement may not be admissible in court."

The lawyer and officers all went outside and huddled for a while. Then they talked to Colleen. The Prosecuting Attorney threatened to charge felonious assault and possession with intent to deliver: a class Y felony with up to 25 years in prison; but William Turner recognized the bluff and started working the possession charge down. Since the marijuana was gift wrapped by someone else and Colleen had merely done a friend a favor, Turner argued, Stapelton should be charged with possession, and not Colleen. After three hours of questioning and wrangling, they finally reached an agreement. All charges would be dropped if Colleen would testify that the marijuana was really Stapelton's and help them find Hot Dog Malone. Colleen refused to testify against Dan, but agreed to help find Malone.

In the end, they charged her with possession of less than a gram of marijuana and released her to Garnet on two thousand dollars bail. It was nine o'clock at night before the exhausted Garnet and Colleen made it home.

—◊◊◊—

Colleen went upstairs to her room, and Garnet was left with being the adult. She checked her messages and heard Mica's baritone voice telling her he had lots to talk about and would try again tomorrow or the day after. Then she picked up the phone and called her sister.

"Hey there. Boy, are you missing out on the fun. These people in Kentucky know how to party!" Rae answered her phone on seeing Garnets ID come up.

"Well, I need you to get your butt out of Kentucky and get here as soon as you can." Garnet was too tired to mince words.

"Hold on there,Little Sis," Rae countered defensively. "What gives?"

"It's Colleen," Garnet sighed. "I just bailed her out of jail."

"Jail? What the hell's going on?"

"She took some marijuana to Mr. Big Man on Campus in the hospital, and he went into convulsions. It could be manslaughter or even murder if he doesn't pull through." Garnet rubbed her forehead absent mindedly as she spoke.

"Shit and carry the two!" Rae exploded. "Where does she think she is, Colorado? I'll leave early in the morning. I've had too much to drink to come now. I should get there by early afternoon. Oh, hell," she continued. "I'm supposed to meet Maezelle in Dallas tomorrow night. Could you put her up too? I'll have her meet me at your place."

"That's fine as long as you two don't mind sleeping in the bunk beds. I'd hate to move Colleen just now. She's pretty shaken."

Next she called her sister Valentine, a February 14th baby, in Greenville, Texas. "I'm sorry," she apologized after filling her in on the day's events. "But this really isn't a good time for Jaxson to visit."

"Oh, that's great news!" Valentine burst out enthusiastically.

Hoping they were having some sort of miscommunication, Garnet took a deep breath. "Great? Would you like to start again?"

"Oh, no," the penitent Valentine stammered. "I didn't mean that what happened was great. I meant that it was great that Jax could go to the Big Bend with his buddy. Charlie's mother just invited him. He was going to pass it up to come see Colleen for a couple of weeks, but now he doesn't have to. Oh my, that didn't come out right either."

"That's all right, Hon. Hopefully it'll all seem better tomorrow."

Garnet checked her watch and unplugged the phone. Her stomach was doing a slow burn, and she really needed some down time.

— ɯ —

Colleen slept the next morning from pure exhaustion. Garnet puttered in the kitchen and stayed close waiting for Colleen to awaken. Garnet wasn't sure how she was going to handle Colleen. She had never known what to do with that child. One minute Colleen was all grown up, and the next minute she was pulling some thirteen year old's stunt. It was as if there were some inborn error of judgment which could not be overcome by a good education and a disciplined environment (She was ever so much like her mother.).

The telephone jarred Garnet from her train of thought. *"Oh dear,"* she thought to herself, *"That's probably some busybody being snoopy. I wonder how long this is going to go on."*

Much to her relief, Sheriff McCurly's ID came up on the phone. "Oh, Curly, it's you. I was afraid it was going to be a reporter or someone. No, Colleen's not up yet. Is there any advice you can give me? I'm not sure what to say to her, you know?"

"Look, Garnet," the Sheriff returned. "We've got problems. I know Colleen doesn't want to testify against the Stapelton kid, but since you found that bottle of pills, we know for a fact he was involved in some pretty risky business. Hattie should have some results late this afternoon. Felony possession alone will put him away for several years. And Colleen is an eye witness. But that's not all, Garnet. We're not just dealing with just a druggie here. We're dealing with a pusher, and Colleen's the only one who can identify him. I'm coming out to talk to her, OK?"

"Well, if you're coming, you'd better get here before her mother does because she will probably kill her!"

Garnet awakened Colleen and told her to dress. When Sheriff McCurly arrived, the three of them sat around the kitchen table and talked.

"Look, Colleen," Curly explained, "I understand your reluctance to incriminate Dan Stapleton. What you did yesterday was noble, but not too bright. No matter what you do, they're still going to deal with Dan. They've got the marijuana, and they've got blood samples, and they've got the phone number from his shoe. Now he may try to blame you, but it's still his gig. And you're going to pay for your part too. But don't fool yourself that if you pay, he won't. That's not the way it works, understand?

"Dan Stapleton is in a heap of trouble," Curly continued. "He denied any knowledge of the bottle when I questioned him. I guess he figured without the bottle we'd never be able to prove he stole anything. A couple of cigarettes over at the hospital are nothing compared to this. We're talking felony possession, even if he did steal it from somebody else. And those folks are in a heap of trouble too."

Colleen turned very pale as she listened to this latest account of events. So Dan had been setting her up all along? She'd fix him. Not with her testimony or anything like that. Even she could see this was serious business. But somewhere down the line he'd slip up, and she'd be there to nail him. Some friend he was!

She looked at Curly and Garnet steadily and asked quietly, "What do you want me to do?"

"Well," Curly began, "there are a couple of things. As I see it, you've got to help us pick up this Hot Dog Malone character as part of your bail agreement. That's number one. Number two, I need you to help me. I won't be able to talk to Dan for at least another day, according to his doctor. He didn't give me much last time. Now we know who the man, Jim Strothers, is. But we suddenly can't find this Edith House woman. She may turn out to be pretty important. It's just possible that she set up the deal to buy in the first place. We've been kind of assuming that Jim was the buyer, right? But then ole Chet didn't seem to balk at handing the stuff over to her according to your story."

Colleen nodded her agreement, "Yeah, I never thought about that. I just assumed Chet, whoever that is, knew both of them. They seemed to kind of be friends or something."

"They're probably all in it together," he reasoned. "How else would Jim's legal prescriptions already be in that cooler? Well, I'll be working on that," Curly returned to his chain of thought.

"Anyway, you and Garnet and I all saw Edith House. I'll send a police artist out. I've already talked to him, but I want both of you to describe her for him. And, Colleen, we need as much as you can remember about Chet and this Hot Dog Malone, OK?"

Colleen bit her lower lip and stared at her lap. Her whole world had caved in yesterday, and she was scared. She'd like to run away. Facing the music was pretty grim. She wanted to help, but what if she screwed up again? This drug stuff was serious business. Somebody could get hurt bad!

12

Dr. Hattie West was busy in her lab. As the Director of MNSU's Program in Forensics, she coordinated what was probably the only interdisciplinary program on campus. Forensics had rapidly become a blend of genetics, biology, biochemistry, chemistry and criminal justice for beginners. The forensics program trained law officers from all over the State in correct procedures and scientific background. Consequently she had attained considerable latitude in analyzing evidence and a budget to go with it.

This afternoon she was carefully analyzing the peaks from the gas chromatograph from the bottle Sheriff McCurly had brought her. Interestingly, the contents were in rather large capsules, not in pills as they had assumed. She had run several chemistry tests and was now refining her data.

She picked up the phone and dialed Curly McCurly's number. She got his voice mail and left a message. Then she began her analysis of the burned joint that Curly had brought her from the hospital. It didn't make sense on the surface that marijuana would have caused the kid's convulsions. It was used by cancer patients who were already on Hydrocodone for pain relief. Although there was some controversy about how effective it really was, it didn't cause convulsions and the symptoms of a heart attack. Could there have been a residue of snake venom in his blood?

She was just finishing up when Sheriff McCurly knocked on the lab door.

She motioned him in and began to talk excitedly. "You'll never believe what I've found. This is a new one on me! First, I analyzed the capsules. There never were any pills. On first examination, I thought the granular patterns were heterogeneous as if the crystals were a mix of some kind. It took me several tries with different solvents, but I finally separated two phases. The first has tested to be Hydrocodone as the label says. But the second was a real surprise: Demerol!"

"Demerol?"

"Yes, we're dealing with a designer drug."

"Demerol?" he asked again. "I thought it was off the market."

"Well," she explained. "It's still being used mainly in hospitals and outside the country. It would be expensive, but it could be smuggled in."

"Now," she continued. "There's the label. It's a very good counterfeit. Notice that the physician's name is really smudged. I think that's on purpose. I ran our syntax program to restore it; it's George Rogers, MD. And guess what? He's dead! And," she pushed on, " I checked with the pharmacy, which is legit, and they don't have a prescription, and the number sequence is last year's. And," she held up her finger to indicate that there was more. "The phone number is 'out of service'."

Curly McCurly was both dumbfounded and amazed. It would have taken the State Crime Lab forever to get these results. Still he had to ask, "No fingerprints?"

"No. Sorry. That really would have been great. Not even a partial."

"Oh, my," the Sheriff thought out loud. "Hydrocodone and Demerol. Wow, that would really be a high! I wonder who thought of that."

"That's not all," she continued. "You were right about the marijuana's not being likely to cause convulsions. But there is another drug that would."

"Don't tell me," he postulated. "The joint's a designer too."

"Oh yes. It's laced with Phenergan with Codeine. Phenergan alone probably wouldn't have done it, but with the extra codeine on top of the Hydrocodone he already had in his system, he didn't have a chance. It's probably there to give an extra punch to the nausea relief, and it should make sleeping lots easier. I'd say it's been designed to boost medical marijuana sales. If the marijuana doesn't knock the nausea, the Phenergan mix will, and the price of the marijuana goes up."

"Any idea where it might have come from?" He asked wearily.

"Not really. I'd guess off hand Colorado or maybe even Washington, but we can't rule out the possibility that it's maybe even local. I hate to say it, but our designers might even be the same."

"Oh, no," the Sheriff groaned. "These things are just like too many babies. We've got to find out where they're coming from."

13

Dan Stapleton floated quietly and painlessly down a long, dark tunnel toward the soft light at the end. He could hear high pitched children's voices calling his name as if to invite him to a game of tag or baseball.

"He's coming, isn't he?" A man's voice asked.

"Yes, yes. He's on his way right now," another answered.

As Dan floated out of the tunnel into the lighted field, he recognized some of the people in the small crowd waiting there for him. There were his grandfather and Uncle Eustes, and there was Mayor Phillips. But they were dead! Was he dead? They beckoned for him to join their friendly smiling group, but while he was attracted by their comforting warmth, something back down the tunnel was beckoning him too, pulling him back. A fatherly voice chided him, "You've got to go back. You still have work to do. You're not finished yet." He fluttered a hand in goodbye to the curious gathering and reentered the tunnel where he began moving faster and faster, as if in a speeding car, back to that other force that called him.

When Dan awakened he was in a hospital room. He recognized one of the nurses and the doctor who had monitored his cardiac function before, but who was that guy in the bed?

"Why, it's me!" he said to himself. *"But why am I here, up above everybody? How can I be in two places at the same time?"*

The doctor finished the examination. "Well, at least he's stabilized," he spoke to the nurse. "He's young and strong, although that snake bite knocked him back a bit. If it had been an older man it probably would have killed him. Nearly did anyway. Oh well, this one won't be playing any football for a while. I don't think his heart can take any more. How's the family holding up? Those folks have sure been through hell. When will these stupid kids learn? If you want to dance, you have to play the fiddler."

Dan watched from his lofty perch as his parents entered the room.

"How is he?" His mother asked the nurse in a soft, strained voice.

"He's stabilized now, Mrs. Stapleton. The doctor thinks he'll pull through. It's mostly a matter of waiting; I know that's been really hard, but it's the best we can do."

Mom nodded her acceptance and approached the young man in the bed. She picked up his hand and stroked it softly. "Dan, Dan," she called in a questioning voice, not quite sure he could hear her. "Dan, can you wake up now sweetheart?"

Dan could feel the dry, warm touch of his mother's hand on his own. He could hear her voice calling softly, pulling him back from wherever he had been. He opened his eyes and blinked at the light. His mother stood on one side of his bed and his father on the other. As he looked at their strained, worried faces, they began to smile with relief, and some of the tension drained from their faces.

"Dan, are you all right?" Mom began wiping tears out of her eyes with the back of her hand. "How do you feel, Son?"

Dan tried to talk, but his throat seemed closed. "Whe... where am I? How did I get back in here?"

His mother looked expectantly at his father. "You smoked some marijuana," his father explained quietly; too quietly. "It interacted with your other medications and affected your heart. You went into convulsions. We weren't sure you were going to make it," he added hollowly.

"What did the doctor say?" Dan asked anxiously. "Am I going to be all right? Am I going to be able to play football? "

"We'll talk about it later," his father said flatly. "I think there's more important things to worry about now, Son."

They kissed him and left the room. Had the doctor been right? Would he never play again? Was that conversation even real, or had he dreamed it? Things were really fuzzy now. Dad seemed mad.

Probably the marijuana. He'd have to be sure they knew Colleen had brought it. Did she still have the cigarettes? How much had she told them? Better keep mum for a while.

Sheriff McCurly waited outside the ICU doors. Dan Stapleton was awake and apparently lucid. He had asked to see Dan shortly after he came out of his first coma following the snake bite. Dan had been uncooperative to say the least. He had claimed he didn't know anything about a bottle of pills. He had wandered into the woods to take a leak and had stepped on a big motherfucker of a snake. He claimed he was so scared, he accidentally ran the wrong way to get help. End of story. The Sheriff knew he was lying, and Dan knew he knew. But Dan was smart. He figured the Sheriff didn't have the bottle, and that even if he did, he'd have a hard time proving possession. Who was going to nail him? Not Jim or Edith; they had too much to lose. Colleen? No. She was such an air head, she'd get her story mixed up, and no one would believe her in the end. It would be her word against his.

"Hello, Dan," Curly began. "I still need to ask you some questions about the bottle of pills you stole. This time Dan went past uncooperative to belligerent, denying his involvement, "I told you I didn't steal any bottle!"

"Well, we think you did."

"Hey, Man, get off my case. If you're so sure there's a bottle, why don't you go find it?"

"We did, Dan. We did. And whose fingerprints are on it, do you think?" Curly bluffed.

Dan turned pale. "I don't know anything about a bottle of pills. And even if you did find one, there's no telling who it belonged to, right?" He dug himself in deeper.

"Now look here, Son," the Sheriff's patience was growing thin. "We know you're involved in this. We don't tolerate drugs in Pope County. You, and who knows how many of your little river party friends, are in for a rude awakening. I'd hoped to talk some sense into you and get you to help us. You almost killed yourself with that marijuana stunt, which, for your information was not just marijuana; it was laced with something (He held back the details.). I bet you don't have any idea what's in those pills. What if they kill somebody else?"

—◊—

Dan dozed fitfully the rest of the afternoon. He was really very tired, but his conscience wouldn't let him sleep. He kept pushing it back, unwilling to admit even to himself that he had screwed up. He eased the gnawing need for self accusation by blaming everyone else. He blamed the football accident for putting him on the river in the first place. Then he blamed Colleen and Hot Dog Malone for being so cooperative. They should have known better than to bring him that stuff in the hospital. Some friends they were. Didn't they know that sick people often asked for things that weren't good for them? And that stupid Colleen wasn't covering for him anymore. The Sheriff knew too much. It had to be Colleen.

Then the inner voice switched to quiet reality. What if those pills were laced with something just like the marijuana had been? Had he dodged a bigger bullet? He was planning to sell them for the big bucks he wanted so badly, but what if they made his customers sick? The Sheriff was going to try to nail him for possession with intent to deliver. What would he have to do to reduce the charge? None of his friends were involved; just those rich pansies from Fayetteville, trying to act like a bunch of college kids. He didn't owe them a thing. Why not try to help? Probably reduce the charge. Maybe there was something in it after all.

—◊—

Dan awakened from a deep sleep later that evening as his father entered the room alone and pulled a chair close to the bed.

"Hi, Dad," Dan offered brightly. "How are things going? Oh, hey, Dad, I'm really sorry about all of this. I know you and Mom have been worried sick. But the doctor says I'm on the mend. I'll be playing football in no time. Don't you worry!"

"Football? No, Son, you're not goin' to be playin' football. What with the snake bite and the marijuana, you've got a bad heart. Oh, you'll make it up and around all right. Probably make it OK at a desk job. But you're not goin' to be playin' football," he said emphatically.

"But, Dad, what about my scholarship? I told Coach I'd be back to play next year. Practice starts in six weeks. They're counting on me!"

"A lot of folks were countin' on you, Son. But it looks like that's just too damn bad! The Sheriff told me what happened down on that river. You nearly got yourself killed stealin' that bottle. And if that wasn't enough, you conned that girl, Colleen, into bringin' you dope in here, in a hospital of all places! Son, when are you goin' to stop thinkin' about yourself and your god dammed football career and start thinkin' about what you're doin' to yourself and everyone who ever cared more than a spit in the ocean about you?

"You came that close," he held his thumb and forefinger together, "to dyin'. Not once, but twice. Why? Because you're hooked on dope and cheap thrills. You done broke your Mother's heart, and you got that Stevens girl in trouble besides. But that's not the worst of it. Son, you've brought shame to your family.

"We're simple folks here, and we raised you with simple values. But just because we're simple, doesn't mean we're stupid. We know what's goin' on out there. We read the papers and watch the news. We know there's dope on almost every corner in the cities. But it shouldn't be that way here. The honest folks that live here don't want dope here. If they wanted dope they'd move. The only people who do dope here are outsiders, folks too lazy to work, and people who've got more money than they've got sense. Sure we've got alcoholics and bums; every town does. But it's not because they were invited. You came in here with your big football scholarship and your fancy friends, and you brought dope in with you. You grew up here, but you don't belong here. If you belonged here, you'd know you don't bring shame in on your own."

Dan's face blushed bright red. He'd never heard his father talk so heatedly or so long. He turned his face away so he wouldn't have to face his father. He heard the chair scraping the floor as the older man stood up and left the room.

Then Dan's face paled as the blood drained from his head and the room began to spin. He had never thought about all this affecting his folks, or how the community would look at him. He had assumed that his football reputation would carry him through. But now that football was gone, his ego suddenly became naked. When you stripped away the football, all that was left was a selfish, doped up jock who scared his folks to death and dragged other people into his messes. His Dad was right. He had been raised better. He'd shamed his folks and his neighbors. He didn't belong here, and he didn't deserve their good will. For the first time in his life he was all alone and scared.

14

After the Sheriff left, Colleen went back up to her room leaving Garnet time to think about the ramifications of Colleen's arrest. She really wished she could talk to Mica. He had very big shoulders and she needed them right now. At least she didn't have to try to make small talk with Colleen.

She heard a car in the driveway and went to the door. Rae was just crawling out of her red Ferrari. She certainly had made good time (The heavy foot ran in the family.). They hugged at the door and without a word Garnet pointed upstairs. Rae took the stairs two at a time, knocked on Colleen's door and disappeared.

It was about an hour before they came down, both looking the worse for wear. Garnet fixed iced tea for all of them and they sat at the table much as she and Colleen had sat with the Sheriff this morning. Was it just this morning? Time was on its own schedule. They made an effort to be positive, completely ignoring the 500 pound joint that was smoldering in the corner. They were saved from themselves by the sound of a car in the driveway. Maezelle to the rescue!

Maezelle Roxy was Rae's business manager and best friend. They traveled together all over the country checking on oil and gas leases and doing their due diligence. Since the Cincinnati trip didn't involve any legal papers, Maezelle had stayed in Dallas to hold down the fort. Besides, the Ferrari didn't have enough room for the amount of luggage these two women usually dragged around.

To Garnet's surprise Maezelle had brought Valentine with her. And why not? Valentine wasn't particularly needed at home since Jaxson was going to the Big Bend, and the load was temporarily light at the legal office where Valentine worked as a paralegal. She also acted as the liaison between Rae and various lawyers in the area who handled Rae's gas and oil deals. She might turn out to be very useful under the current circumstances.

Maezelle rushed past both Garnet and Rae and swept Colleen into a big hug. "Oh, Darlin'" she drawled. "How in the world are y'all? When your Momma told me what had happened, I couldn't get my mind around it! My little rodeo queen a smokin' pot. Whatever is goin' to happen next?"

"Uh, Aunt Maezelle," Colleen dipped her chin. "I wasn't really the one smoking. I know you don't like to think so, but I really screwed up. I got arrested because I did something really stupid, and I know it. No excuses."

"Oh, no!" Rae screeched from her side of the table. "They didn't." She read from the local paper which showed an unflattering mug shot of her daughter. "Colleen Stevens was arrested yesterday for possession of less than one ounce of marijuana. According to the Sheriff's deputy who responded to the third floor of St. Mary's Hospital, Stevens had supplied a patient with marijuana, allegedly at his request.' ALLEGEDLY?" she ranted. "And where is the name of the male patient? How come she's taking all the heat? It goes on to say how much bail was."

"That's standard treatment," Garnet explained. "Some days there's a whole page of mug shots."

They were interrupted by Sheriff McCurly's phone call giving Garnet the report from Hattie. "Now I know your sister is coming in, but let me remind you that this is still under investigation, and you are required to keep this information confidential. One little statement outside of your house, and I'll have to revoke Colleen's bail."

The four women talked among themselves openly now. They acknowledged the severity of the problem and began trying to figure out possible leads. Where had Chet come from? How did he get Jim's prescriptions to put into the red cooler? How was Edith House involved? Was she a pusher or a mule? Who was Hot Dog? Was he a Russellville resident? Who were the designers, and where did they mix their pharmaceuticals?

When they finally ran out of steam, Rae offered to take Colleen for a ride in the Ferrari. "I'll even let you drive," she promised.

Maezelle was quick to move on to something else too. Why waste time spinning your wheels? "Garnet, I've just got ta know if y'all have any haunted houses around here. I started ghost bustin' just for fun about a year ago, and I swear it's better than sex! Well sometimes anyway. I brought all my gear since I was travelin' by myself. There's not enough room in that Ferrari to pack a Kotex."

"Well as a matter of fact we do," Garnet was happy to help. Anything to ease the worry. "There's an old Victorian house back behind the campus. The kids tell all kinds of tales about seeing giant animals there at night. It's for sale. I know a good real estate agent who could probably get you in. Interested?"

She called Janis Haynes and made arrangements for her to meet Maezelle later that afternoon, then drew a map for Maezelle who left early to check out the area.

Janis was really helpful and really chatty. The house was called Mulberry Hall. It was owned by a doctor in town, a psychiatrist who lived in an enormous Victorian mansion with a third story ballroom back up the hill toward the river. It had belonged to his aunt who left it to him. He had rented it for a while, but found the repairs and monitoring to be too much of a hassle, so he had put it on the market. But with the economy he was having a hard time selling it even though it was so close to the university. The local kids claimed it really was haunted, and it had become an attractive nuisance. If Maezelle could get some photos of whoever was really scaring the kids, it would make it easier to sell. And a nice commission would certainly come in handy!

She offered Maezelle a key to the lock box and wished her good luck.

15

When Maezelle came back to the house, Garnet was just coming out of the bathroom. "I didn't want to teach this summer so I could get some rest," she complained. "Now look at me. I'm spending half my time in the bathroom and living on simethicone. Go figure. Radar Rae just called. They're up at Fayetteville and not coming in for dinner. They're having bar-b-que. Guess that's comfort food for you Texans," she laughed.

"Sure is," Maezelle responded. "Look why don't y'all just take a nap? I've got to get my gear set up for a ghost hunt, and I can grab a bite in town. I'm hungry for Texas' other comfort food, Mexican, and you don't need it with your insides all torn up like that."

"Well, it's not all that bad," Garnet hedged. "But you do have a point, and a nap sounds heavenly right now." She turned to Valentine, "There's left over pizza if you want it." Valentine nodded, and Garnet headed for bed.

"Fine. I'll see you later tonight with some good ghost stories." She went out to her car and retrieved a large blue rolling bag full of various cameras tape recorders, trip wires, etc. This was going to be great! All she had to do was wait for dark.

Maezelle was excited about the prospects of catching a "ghost". She had a whole album of night photos showing everything from cats and rats to young lovers, kids and human rats from her various escapades. It was still a thrill for her to document the ghosts of old houses.

She parked her classic emerald green Thunderbird in a back lot at the college and trudged down one hill then back up another to the house. She entered quietly using her borrowed key and began to set up her cameras and trip wires and voice activated tape recorders with as little light as possible.

Meanwhile Dr. Francis (Frank) Norton was trying to catch a breeze out on the widow's walk of his own house when he saw a flicker of light at the house down the hill.

"Drat!" he said to himself. *"Not again!"* He really wanted to sell the house, not set it up as a playhouse for the local miscreants. Renting had been too much hassle for him, but selling it was almost as bad. He had already painted the living room twice to cover the graffiti various trespassers had scrawled on the walls.

He climbed down to the third floor and took the elevator to the first floor where his office and reception room were located. He rummaged in one of the closets for some supplies then started down the hill by the pale light of the moon.

Maezelle had just finished setting up the camera on the fireplace mantle when she heard a sound coming from the back of the house. She turned off her light and stepped back. Just then the door to the back hallway crashed open. She quickly turned her light back on and saw a giant white rabbit! She screamed and dropped her flashlight which rolled all the way across the floor into the far corner, well out of reach.

"What are you doing here?" they yelled at each other in unison.

When neither answered, they simultaneously scrambled for the light switch behind the door, crashing into each other and knocking Maezelle to the floor. To her horror the white rabbit whose head had been knocked around until he couldn't see, grabbed for her blindly and caught the front of her bloused tearing off two or three buttons. She screamed again just as the ceiling light came on.

She crouched on the floor fully expecting to be attacked when the rabbit took his head off. "Geeze it's hot in here," Frank complained.

"Hot in here? Is that all you have to say? You nearly scared me to death!" She stood up and stretched all of her five feet-three inches in indignation.

"And, you...you," he stammered realizing he didn't have much dignity left with his disheveled hair and a rabbit's head in his hand. "You're trespassing. This is my house, and this is my rabbit, and I plan to keep both of them!"

"Janis Haynes gave me a key so I could look for ghosts," she informed him. "Wait a minute. Did you say this is your house? Are you the doctor?"

"Yes, I am, that is when I'm not a rabbit," he tried to keep a straight face.

"Oh, I'm so sorry," they said to each other in unison before breaking out into loud laughter.

"I thought you were a graffiti artist."

"I thought you were a raping rabbit."

When they had finished laughing and had caught their breath, Frank made an overture, "It really is hot in here. Why don't you come up to the house with me and we'll sit out on the veranda and watch the river? There's usually a good breeze this time of night."

Maezelle smiled her acceptance and began to collect her gear. As she retrieved the flashlight from the corner, she saw something white glistening in the light. She looked closer and saw a large medicine capsule. "Oh, my," she chortled. "I think we really have found our ghost!"

They carried her gear and the rabbit's head to her car then drove up to the old mansion where they sipped iced tea and started the "getting to know you" game. She was especially pleased when he encouraged her to come back during the day next week when his wife would be back from California. Maezelle wouldn't have minded if Frank had been single, but she had learned through the years that a good male friend is harder to find than a lover. Besides she needed to get her find back to Garnet's.

—◊◊—

Rae, Colleen, Valentine and Garnet were out on the veranda enjoying a rare night breeze when Maezelle returned with her amazing find. They immediately moved inside to their around-the-table positions, and Garnet called Sheriff McCurly who sighed with fatigue but rounded up Deputy Dawson (also called Deputy Dawg) who would be leading the local investigation and made the short drive out to the house.

The six of them sat around the table trying to figure out just what was the significance of the capsule and how to proceed from here. Clearly someone had been in the house with what looked to be the same drug. But who? Was it the designer, the pusher or maybe a customer?

What they needed was some surveillance on that house. But then Deputy Dawson said there wasn't any available overtime this month or until the end of June when the next Qorum Court deposit was made; and besides it was simply too hot to post lookouts. Sheriff McCurly lamented that they didn't have enough functioning wireless video equipment which would be needed to avoid detection. Once again, Maezelle came to the rescue.

"Well," she drawled, "I have an idea. When I was in Florida for a ghost hunters convention, I met this man." Then she quit talking as if the others knew what that meant.

"Aaaand?" Rae prompted. She'd been around Maezelle long enough to know she often stopped in mid sentence while she thought about details.

"His name was Sammy Slater," Maezelle continued. "He was, or I should say is, an electronics and robotics expert. He works for Disney designing and setting up animatronics."

"OK, I'll bite, Rae conceded. "What are animatronics?"

"Well," Maezelle continued. "Y'all know all those talking and moving figures at Disney World?" The others nodded their recognition of the subject. "Well, he designs those. But more important, he designs all sorts of little critters that have microphones and cameras inside of them."

"You're kidding." Deputy Dawson burst out. They have surveillance down there? You mean those cute little mice are taking pictures?"

"Well, of course, silly," Maezelle was not intimidated by his badge, although she did think he looked mighty nice in that uniform shirt. "They have cameras out on the corners of the concourses, but what if you get robbed in the Tunnel of Love?"

At that they all laughed as if to say, "Been there; done that."

"And the best part is he's from Texas," Maezelle continued as the others tried to figure out how one person in several million Texans would be a great find. "Anyway, when he found out I was from Texas too, we really hit it off. He showed me some of his animal animatronics, and I swear they looked real. Sooo, if we could get him to come up here, he could set up our surveillance."

"Sounds great," Sheriff McCurly interjected. "But if we don't have money for overtime, we sure don't have money to hire this guy to come up here."

"Oh, I think he'll come for free, or for such a small amount that Rae can pay it," Maezelle assured him.

"Rae can pay it? Why me?"

"Because it's your daughter, and you have more money than I do," Maezelle stated matter -of-factly.

"We'll talk about this later," Rae rejoined. "How soon can you get in touch with him?"

"He gave me his cell number, so I could call him first thing in the mornin' and set it up. What are the rest of y'all goin' to do?"

They talked again for some time before deciding that surveillance alone wouldn't result in the information or evidence they needed. What they needed was a sting. So tomorrow morning Maezelle would call Sammy; Deputy Dawson would take the capsule to Hattie West to verify that it was the same as the others; and Sheriff McCurly would have a long chat with Dan Singleton about his responsibilities to the community (and a possible reduction in his penalties).

When the Sheriff and Deputy Dawson got up to leave, Maezelle made a special point of seeing them to the door. The Deputy wasn't wearing a wedding band, and she was interested in learn-ing more. They flirted a little at the door while the Sheriff waited patiently. Then she came back to see the others grinning knowingly and passing the M&Ms.

16

Chet, Conner and Hot Dog, whose real name was Royce, sat in the prep room of "The Lodge" tallying the week's receipts and discussing their strategy. "Man," Hot Dog asked excitedly, "what did you put in that weed? That knocked ole Dan flat on his ass. They put him back in ICU. We've got to be careful with that stuff!"

"Yeah, too bad about that," Chet stated calmly even though he didn't feel calm at all. *What if Dan had actually died?* "That was some of our best stuff with a little Phenergan (*actually quite a lo*t) added. We were hoping to market it as medicinal marijuana. That way it knocks down the nausea even further. It should have been a great seller. It's a good thing we hit ole Dan first. He was really doped up on Hydrocodone. And a lot of cancer patients who would be our medical marijuana customers take some pretty hefty doses of the stuff. We'd have literally <u>killed</u> our market if a bunch of them went into convulsions and clocked out on us."

"No lie, Man," Hot Dog responded. "Let's scratch that as a failed 'clinical trial'". They all laughed. "You got any other ideas in the works?"

"Do I have any other ideas? Surely you jest. Conner and I took some of that last batch of Hydrocodone and blended it with a little Demerol. Talk about a sweet ride!"

"You bet," Conner smiled happily.

"I don't get it, guys." Hot Dog looked puzzled. "Don't both of those drugs use the same receptors?" He was learning the lingo quickly.

"That's the beauty of it," Chet explained. "When you start taking it, every receptor in your brain gets hit, kind of like cocaine. You're going to get hooked in no time, while the price keeps going up, I might add. Then when the receptors downshift, the two drugs start competing, and you can never get the same ride unless you lay off for two or three months."

"But what will the 'customer' do?" Conner continued. "He'll keep buying even larger amounts trying for the same feeling. And our sales will go up, and our profits will go up!"

"Was that what was in the lost bottle?" Hot Dog wasn't going to let that episode fade away.

"Yeah, damn it!" Chet spoke disgustedly. "Edith was going to take some up to Fayetteville. Those guys up there will try anything."

"Did you protect her?" Hot Dog pressed.

"Of course I did!" Chet snapped. "We ran the labels on three legitimate prescriptions for Jim then copied the phony one as Guafinesen."

"Thank God for small favors," Hot Dog sighed. "Lord knows where that bottle is. Anyone who finds it will probably just throw it away. Thanks for making that delivery for me. I really had a bad case of the shits. There was no way you could have known what Dan was up to."

Chet was feeling a little paranoid. Was Hot Dog being honest, or trying to psych him out?

"Got to run," Hot Dog stood up. "Maybe I can stay and try your double blend next time."

Conner walked him up the stairs and out the back then came to sit across from Chet. "Bad luck, huh?"

"Yeah, yeah," Chet grumbled then spoke in a high voice aping Hot Dog. "There was no way you could have known what Dan was up to."

"Give it a rest, OK?" Conner grumbled back. "So far they've kept their end of the deal. And you know we've built in some protection."

Chet and Conner were the main producers in the group, and Hot Dog was their main salesman. There were only one or two others who ever handled the product, and, except for Edith, the only person they had met was Hot Dog. The threesome felt it was important to keep the inside group very small. Everybody around here was related to any number of persons who might be and probably were gossips. The main relationship in this group was between Hot Dog and their major funder whom they simply called The Big One. The other two had been forced to take on Hot Dog as part of the deal; clearly he was there to keep an eye on them. And that certainly contributed to Chet's paranoia.

Taking on Hot Dog had proved to be gold in the bag. He was an agent for Sweet Home Realty which was owned by his mother. The two of them knew everybody in Pope and Yell counties and traveled all over the State. Hot Dog used the guise of showing houses to make his sales, and sometimes he even sold the house. They had set up drop boxes out of the area for their weed and meds. When Hot Dog went to a realty meeting in, say Jonesboro, he picked up supplies on the way back. Since he was taking the risk of transporting unlicensed meds, he cut out one big headache for the other two.

Chet and Conner had gone to MNSU together and had been roommates at pharmacy school where they had shared the thrill of trying several designer drugs that other students had cooked up. They had gone to different areas of the State to work, but had stayed in touch. After a particularly pricy Marijuana buy from Hot Dog, Chet had been contacted by an anonymous "benefactor" who had suggested that funding was available for local designer work if Chet could find himself a pharmacist partner.

Of course Chet had blown it off. No way anyone was going to set him and a buddy up in business. It was either a joke or a sting, and he was too smart to be taken in by either. However, after his third purchase of some righteous weed, Hot Dog casually mentioned that there was a message in the bag.

Chet's blood raced when he saw the number suggested as his share of the take. It had to be a setup. Didn't it? But how could the Fifth Judicial Drug Task Force afford to bait him at that rate? He'd have to make the product before they could arrest him. That meant an elaborate yet highly secretive lab plus a lot of expensive drugs. No, it was too pricy for the locals. This was coming from someone else. Maybe he really should look into it. This could make him enough to refurbish his old Victorian house in Atkins in high style. Besides, simply showing up for a meet couldn't hurt anything. It would all be perfectly innocent on his part. If he got busted he would simply claim he was gathering data to turn over to the Drug Task Force.

17

When Sammy Slater arrived, it was easy for Garnet to see why Maezelle and Sammy had hit it off. He was bigger than life, and she was tougher than leather. They both had Texas written all over them. Sammy rolled in from Disney World in a shining white Ford F-150 4x4 with all the bells and whistles. Talk about a knight in shining armor! Alas, fair maidens, he was taken by a very savvy physician who specialized in pediatrics.

Sammy climbed down from his 'trusty steed', and Maezelle introduced him around. After shaking hands with everyone and perusing the menagerie of vehicles in the parking area, he observed, "You ladies sure do have good taste in vehicles. I figured with the Texas connection you'd all be driving Chryslers and Caddies."

"Caddies!" Rae snorted, "Nobody who has any <u>real</u> money drives a Caddie."

"Your point is well taken," he smiled back at her. "I'm guessing you're driving the Ferari. You strike me as a lady who likes adventure. And let me see, Maezelle that T-Bird would be yours; the Mustang would be Colleen's. And that leaves the Dakota with purple fire to you," he nodded toward Garnet.

"You've got it," Garnet laughed. "I guess we could have our own car show out here in my parking area. Meanwhile, do come in and freshen up before we get started on another kind of show."

They quickly told Sammy about what they needed for their surveillance mission, and he went to his truck and began pulling some things out just to show them how the system would work. His favorite animatron was a saucy squirrel that charmed them all with his cheeky attitude and swishy tail that was controlled remotely. But they were blown away with the motion-detector skunk that turned its back and lifted its tail ready for a spray.

"Is that real?" Colleen squeeked.

"Nah, not really," Sammy explained. "He has a perfume sprayer built in, but I don't think that will do you any good out in the woods."

"OK, this is the way it works," Sammy continued, quite serious now. "As soon as we get the permits for photos and recordings, we can begin setting up. We'll set up the inside with voice activated cameras and recorders. That will give us a good idea who has been there and what was going on. The outside will be a little more difficult. We'll put the skunk at the back to try to make sure everybody comes in from the front. We don't want any surprises. Then we'll set up some more cameras in the bushes and flower beds. But the *piece de resistance* is Merlin-the-Squirrel."

"Merlin?" they asked in unison.

"Well, I couldn't very well name him 'Sammy-the-Squirrel', now could I?"

"OK, so what does Merlin do?" Rae took the bait.

"Merlin is remote controlled; that means some-one has to be there to operate him. Unless you want to sit out in the hot woods 24 hours a day, you'll have to plan ahead a little. What he does will really be a help though. Do you have anything metal handy?" He asked Garnet.

She looked around and spotted the wheel bar-row plant stand near the door, raising her eyebrows in question.

"Perfect," Sammy approved. Then he took a small three-inch square box from Merlin's tool box and fitted it to Merlin's right front paw. He moved a joy stick and Merlin scampered toward the wheel barrow then ducked under it. Sammy manipu-lated the control, and when Merlin reappeared, the box was gone from his paw. "There!" Sammy exclaimed, "You have just witnessed the attach-ment of a GPS tracking device to the underside of Garnet's 'vehicle'."

"Sweet!" the women exclaimed in unison. "Let me try it."

"Now, now, ladies. You'll have to take turns," Sammy admonished. "There's a good bit of skill in ejecting the magnet on the tracker. If it's done wrong, the whole shebang will stick to the car, and poor little Merlin could be dragged to his death.

You'll need to pick your remote operator so we can go over the sequence several times before we set the system up." After some bickering, they agreed that Maezelle should do the honors since it was her idea and her friend. Although the others made her agree they'd all get their shot later.

—⁊⁊⁊—

There were still a few days before the trap could be sprung. Dr. Norton had agreed to the photography and taping. Under Arkansas law the owner of a property had to give permission for photography on the premises before any photos could be used legally; and at least one of the participants in a conversation had to be aware when any taping was occurring. Dan Singleton had agreed reluctantly to bait the trap. He would call Jim and offer to sell the pills for $1,000. The whole transaction would be photographed and recorded while Maezelle attached the GPS tracker. However, a tracker had to be court approved and that would take several days. The fact that Mulberry Hall was in Yell County was not a major obstacle, since both Pope and Yell Counties were partners in the Fifth Judicial Task Force.

Early the next morning Sammy and Maezelle went out to Mulberry Hall to find a place for Maezelle to set up. It was important that she be able to plant the tracker quickly and in the dark.

After helping set up all the equipment inside the house and the skunk at the back door, Sammy was on his way back to Florida, leaving Maezelle to practice from behind a cover of dense lilac bushes.

She called Sweet Home Realty and told Janis Haynes she was setting up more equipment but should be finished in about a week, so that any realtor who showed the house would not be concerned if she were there. Then she headed back to Garnet's and spent the afternoon planting GPS trackers under all the cars and trucks. As dusk gathered, she headed back for night practice.

18

When the court order hadn't come in, the ladies began to get fidgity. So Rae went out to examine and learn more about Arkansas shale, specifically the Fayetteville shale play with Dr. Carly Becker, MNSU's head geologist. After the pair had driven off in Dr. Becker's old International Scout, Maezelle and Valentine set out to practice with Merlin, and Garnet called to make the promised lunch appointment with Stephanie Gleason. As it happened, today was perfect.

Stephanie was already seated when Garnet arrived at The Mexican Border, a local watering hole with excellent Tex-Mex food. They exchanged greetings as Garnet was seated. She noticed a third menu and water glass across the table. "I knew you wouldn't mind," Stephanie explained. "I invited Olivia Hubbard; she just got back into town Sunday, and I'm dieing to hear what she did in Australia!"

"No, not at all," Garnet agreed. "She's always good company. Meanwhile how is our patient doing?" meaning the big black snake.

"Well, he's still shedding lots of skin, but I think he's going to make it. I'll need to keep him until he eats and digests something before I can be sure."

Garnet was really relieved. She couldn't explain why the fate of the snake meant so much to her, but she clearly cared. Maybe it was something primitive.

Olivia Hubbard arrived just a few minutes later. "Hi, you two," she bubbled. "It's so good to see both of you!"

"How was your trip?" Stephanie prompted as they scanned their menus.

"Oh, it was wonderful! We had three baby emus hatch while I was there. I hated to leave them, but I needed to get back to our farm here, and my Dad hasn't been doing so well. He's been falling lately and having trouble getting up. He said not to worry. He'd just lie there and take a nap until he had enough strength to get up. Can you believe?"

"My dad did that too, the falling that is," Stephanie offered. "We finally had to get someone to stay with him full time. He was adamant that he didn't want to go to a home, and he seemed to really enjoy the company. He always had an eye for the fairer sex."

They ordered their lunch then continued their conversation. "So, Olivia," Garnet asked facetiously, " do you have enough to keep you busy for a while?" Olivia was married to an Australian whose family had deep roots in the emu industry. They had traveled internationally promoting emu farms and helping set up local organizations. Her husband was currently president of Emu International. When Olivia's dad had started going down hill, she bought a fantastic horse farm outside Dover and converted it to emus. She flew back and forth to Australia and kept an eye on her dad who lived in his own house in Russellville. Her dad was getting frailer, and she was spending more time Stateside.

"Brandon (our foreman) manages beautifully without me. He does just about everything except pay the bills. Funny how that works. I'm really excited though. We're going down to Heifer International next week to see if we can help them work emus into their plans somewhere. They may be too exotic, 'read pricey'," she held up her fingers to make quotes.

Their meals came, and they continued chatting while they ate. Garnet loved visiting with professional women. They didn't feel obligated to stay on safe topics when they were together.

When Garnet came home she was met with a calm silence. Colleen had been called in to work and the others were still out. Only then did she realize how tired she was. This drug thing was starting to pull her down and make her a little blue. However, she perked up when she saw the email from Mica.

Garnet, Things are going very well here this week. I flew out of Ben Gurion Airport to Eilat yesterday. Dr. Greene took me to the Last Refuge for dinner. I'm afraid I waddled back to the hotel. The seafood was wonderful! We're going out into the field tomorrow. There were a few rockets from Gaza over the weekend, but none so far this week. Solly and I went to see the world's largest wooden rocking horse in Kadima over the weekend. It can seat up to 26 children at once. It's in the Guiness World Records. Hope the ruckus with the drugs has died down at your end. I miss you. Eat some M&Ms for me. Love you, Mica

Garnet laughed out loud when she opened the JPG attachment. There was the world's largest rocking horse with about 10 children and, almost in the middle, her brother-in-law Sol! He was grinning and holding his arms up in triumph, clearly the biggest child having the most fun.

The laugh calmed her nattering mind, and she was able to enjoy a nice afternoon nap assisted by Fred Astair. The sound of voices in the kitchen woke her up, and she was surprised to see it was almost dark.

Rae and Carly had just returned with two large Papa Murphy's pizzas and salad, and Valentine was busy setting the oven while Mazelle nursed a DosXX. Rae was really excited. "Garnet," she exclaimed, "this woman really knows her shale. Did you know she actually wrote an important paper on how to stop road cuts from falling and sliding into the road? But did they listen? No. We were stuck in one lane traffic on I-540 up by Fayetteville while they hauled shale away."

"But I thought Fayetteville shale had gas in it," Garnet said hesitantly knowing she was missing something.

"It does," Carly explained. "But the shale up I-540 is what they call Atoka shale. It's mostly clay on shale. And when it's cut through a slanted area, the rain washes it out, and you get landslides. They've had to haul in tons of limestone to stabilize the cuts. My paper showed that most cuts in that area were too steep and almost guaranteed to fail. But, it makes more jobs for somebody," she added facetiously.

After their pizza, Garnet turned on the Weather Channel to check on the next day's weather. "Yikes," Valentine exclaimed. "That storm looks as if it's coming straight toward us out of Clarksville!" Carly hurried toward home, and they all scrambled to secure the trash cans and lawn chairs before it hit. Rae texted Colleen at work to tell her to stay put until the storm had passed. Some of Russellville's streets were prone to flooding during a good downpour.

The group rushed to unplug computers and major appliances. The house had lightening rods and a whole-house-surger, but lightening had been known to blow holes in houses in the area. The storm put on a fantastic lightening show which impressed them all, but not Fred Astair. He ran under the bed and stayed.

19

The next morning they all went outside to assess the damage. Several shingles were missing along the edge of the house, and an old sweet gum had been blown over close to the work shop.

Garnet was just about to call Dixon's Tree Service when the phone rang. It was Olivia Hubbard. "Garnet," she said hurriedly, "I hate to call, but I really need help. A tree fell over the back fence sometime during the storm, and four of our female emus got out. We're really short handed, and I would be ever so grateful if you could come help hunt for them or give me the name of someone else to call."

"Let me call you back in just a little bit."

Garnet conferred with the others who agreed to come along to help. Garnet called back to reassure Olivia. Then they gathered up long pants and long-sleeved shirts, bug spray, water, and peanut butter and jelly sandwiches in backpacks and crammed into the Dakota for the trip. They all had cell phones with GPS, but Garnet cautioned them that as you went further north in Pope County you encountered fewer towers and more hills, so that cell phones were not very useful. However they could still take pictures to follow back like bread crumbs if they got lost.

"Oh great," Maezelle quipped. "Now were playing Hanzel and Gretel."

Garnet followed her road back out to Hwy 7 and headed north through Dover, and turned left on 164 passing Booger Hollow and crossing the twin bridges over the Piney. Then she turned right onto a gravel road and traveled almost a mile to a narrow turnoff on the right. About a quarter mile of bumping led them to a lovely house and barns surrounded by white fences that had once confined horses. Now the fences were backed with 6 foot wire mesh to keep emus in.

Olivia had been watching for them and stepped out onto the deep front porch. "I am so sorry to drag you out here," she apologized. "But three of our workers are caught with their own storm problems. Horace is having to cut his way out of his driveway, and the other two are trying to get tarps over their roofs before more rain gets here."

They reassured her they were ready to go to work. She handed them each hand-drawn maps and oriented them toward north. The foreman and one helper had gone south to try to stop the emus before they got back to the main road. Hopefully "the girls" would not try to cross the Piney which was banked with steep ravines just east of the property. Once you got into the Ozark National Forest, the little roads began branching into old logging roads. There weren't very many houses back in there, so Olivia suggested they make good notes on their maps in case they got lost.

Olivia tried to imitate the moomff, moomff sounds of the emus and warned them not to get too close if they found them. Emus had a very strong forward kick that could do some bodily harm. If they found them, the hunters should return to the farm for help.

They piled back into the Dakota and went back to the "good" gravel road following it north until it branched. They split up then and went in on foot.

Valentine and Maezelle headed vaguely westward marking every branch and path on their maps. When they came to a little narrow road with tire tracks they tried to follow it, but the mud-holes were so wide they were forced to veer off into the woods to get around them more often than not.

"I can't believe anyone would want to live back here," Maezelle complained.

"Well," Valentine explained, "lots of folks around here value their privacy. There are a lot of old hillbillies around here that, as my mother would say, are 'funny turned'. They aren't very highly socialized and they'd just as soon keep to themselves."

After about an hour of wandering around various paths, they stopped in a little clearing to rest and have a snack. The bottled water tasted wonderful! They sat on a giant oak log to have their peanut butter sandwiches. Maezelle was half way through her sandwich when she felt a tapping on her back. She glanced over her shoulder to see a furry appendage stretching toward her ear. "YEEOW!" she screamed at the top of her lungs as sandwich, water bottle, and map went flying through the air. The scream startled Valentine who was amazed at how far Maezelle could jump in just one leap.

"What's wrong? What's wrong?" Valentine was panicked thinking of the possibility of snake bite.

"That, that, that," Maezelle stuttered pointing toward the log where a large fox squirrel was nonchalantly chomping on the discarded sandwich.

"He just wanted to be invited to lunch," Valentine sputtered between peals of laughter.

Maezelle didn't think it was very funny until the first shot of adrenalin passed. Then she started laughing too. They'd stop laughing for a few seconds then start again until they were almost laughed out.

"Oh, my," Valentine giggled. "I've got to go pee. I'll wet myself if I laugh any more."

"Me too," Maezelle agreed.

They found some protective bushes and watching for snakes and poison ivy completed their business. As they returned to the log to collect what the squirrel had left, Valentine speculated that there must be a house near because the squirrel was used to being fed. That's when they both heard a soft moomff, moomff to their right behind some trees.

They walked very carefully toward the sound which grew louder as they approached. They were surprised to find all four "ladies" wandering around in the front yard of a badly neglected white house eating the flowers off the old florabunda roses that clung to the remnants of an old chain link fence.

"We found them!" they both blurted out then clamped hands over their mouths and looked at each other hoping they hadn't spooked the big birds. The emus simply looked up then continued defoliating the premises.

The two women walked very slowly around the outside of the yard taking several pictures before they hurried down the muddy road back toward the farm. It wasn't until they came across their own footprints as they skirted a giant puddle that they realized they had been on this road before. They had come full circle thanks to the great squirrel mishap.

Garnet and Rae were worn out. They had walked all afternoon looking for emus down muddy ruts of narrow little "roads" leading to houses and cabins on the Piney. They had made it back to the "main" gravel road when they heard a vehicle coming up behind them. To their surprise a park ranger in uniform darted out of the bushes about 20 yards ahead of them and plopped a soda can directly in the middle of the narrow road. Then he dashed up the road another 30 yards and disappeared back into the bushes.

The bearded driver of an old Ford pickup stopped beside them and offered a ride. The cab was filled with a toothless woman and two half dressed kids. Tired as they were, they just couldn't bring themselves to hop into the back with the manure and dogs. They thanked the man and started walking again.

As the truck straddled the soda can, the park ranger jumped out from the bushes ahead and waved his arms wildly to stop the truck while he shouted gleefully, "Left of center! Left of center!"

He proceeded to write out a ticket for the protesting driver for traveling left of center on an improved federal road.

"But there ain't no center on this road," the man argued incredulously.

"You see that can back there?" the ranger pointed. "That's the center of the road. I marked it myself!"

"Well, I'll be contestin' this you can bet for sure."

The ranger smiled politely, all business now. "Sir, you certainly have the right to do so. Traffic court is held in Little Rock the third Friday of each month. You can take your complaint there. Or, you can mail in the fine with a money order or a certified check."

"Little Rock?" the man could hardly believe what he was hearing.

"Oh yes, this road is on federal land, and all traffic complaints have to be filed in Little Rock."

"Well I ain't payin' no fine !"

"Very well. Suit yourself. Have a nice day, Sir. And please pay attention to your driving." The

ranger stepped back from the truck and disappeared into the woods leaving the very confused
driver to continue on his way hugging the right side
of the road.

Garnet and Rae trudged on down the road in
disbelief. Then they started laughing and running
across the road in diagonal crisscrosses while they
giggled, "Left of center! Left of center!"

When they got back to the truck, they found a
note on the windshield to come back to the farm. It
wasn't a very long ride, but it was a taste of heaven.

Olivia insisted that they stay for a dinner of
grilled emu, corn on the cob, a garden salad, and, of
course, guacamole and chips. They had never eaten
emu before and found they really liked it.

By the time they reached home, the two in the
back of the Dakota were sound asleep.

They all just wanted to shower and put their
carcasses to bed. However they all perked up when
they heard the voice on the message machine.

"This is Sheriff McCurly. The court order has
been signed. Let's meet tomorrow, say 9:00 in my
office, to finalize our plan. Hope you ladies had a
nice day."

20

The gang was up early and chomping at the bit about the possibility (a done deal in their minds) of catching a drug dealer. However, only Garnet and Maezelle were actually supposed to attend the Sheriff's briefing on the sting.

Sheriff McCurly also had an air of anticipation about him when they arrived. Dan Stapleton was there, ankle bracelet and all. Dan's first task this morning had been to call Jim in Fayetteville to set up a meet at Mulberry Hall if possible for tonight. He had left a cryptic message, and they were waiting for a call. When Dan's phone began playing fight song music, they all jumped and huddled closer to hear. The deal was a straight forward exchange of $1,000 in $20's for the bottle. No questions asked. No extra people along. Dan knew where to get a key. They agreed on a 9:30 meeting time. The cover of darkness had advantages for both of them.

Maezelle would go out about dusk to check the recording and photo equipment then set up Merlin. She would park her car up the Hill at Dr. Norton's then walk back down the path in plenty of time. In fact she'd have over an hour to fight off bugs and drive herself crazy going over the plan. The Sheriff and one or two men would also be in the woods to serve as backup in case something went wrong.

The women ate and drank and ate some more trying to wear the day into night. They worked on a jig-saw puzzle Garnet had set out in the dining room table. Garnet, Rae and Valentine always worked puzzles together as part of their annual Christmas ritual. They could drink wine and chat as the puzzle progressed. No wine today; maybe later tonight. The puzzle was a herd of zebras, and they were soon bitching and gnashing their teeth trying to sort out all the stripes.

Finally, the sun began to set and Maezelle headed for Mulberry Hall. She went inside and checked the automatic equipment then made sure Merlin was working and all the batteries were charged. Following a short drive up the hill and a brief wait that seemed too long, she walked back down the path, skirting the skunk, and taking up her post behind the lilacs.

At 9:15 Sheriff McCurly climbed out of the unmarked Ford that was also parked at Mulberry Hall as if Dan had driven it. He removed Dan's ankle bracelet and handed him a bottle identical to the one that was locked away in evidence. Then the Sheriff disappeared into the night.

Dan quickly climbed the two steps to the porch, opened the lockbox and unlocked the door. Nervously, he waited for Jim outside. There were too many ways this could get messed up; the tight end was as nervous as if this were a football game for the championship. He was feeling like vomiting when a car pulled up at 9:35. It was too dark to see the driver, but Dan waited until he was on the steps before he reached inside the door to flip on the lights then stepped inside.

Outside Maezelle was busy directing Merlin toward the back of the car which was all she could make out from the weak lighting coming through the windows without risking being seen.

Dan was absolutely shocked when he looked at Jim. It wasn't Jim. It was Edith House!

"You again, you little bastard!" she snarled at him. "Do you have my bottle?"

"Do you have my money?" He tried not to let her see how shaken he was.

She reached inside a pocket and pulled out a wad of $20's which she held out at arm's length. He reciprocated by holding the bottle out toward her. Cautiously they exchanged the money and drugs.

Dan counted the $20's while Edith opened the bottle. The money was all there. "Son of a bitch!" Edith exploded flinging the bottle of caplets onto the floor and grabbing her money back. "Who the hell do you think you are, you little piss ant, trying to double cross me?"

Dan was taken completely by surprise as she rushed out the door, climbed into her car and roared back toward the highway. Fortunately Merlin had just planted the GPS tracker. Although he was still under the car, he just missed being smushed, and startled Maezelle who wet herself in the dark.

Sheriff Wilson materialized out of the dark to collect Dan. "Well, son you've earned your freedom," he informed Dan as he threw the ankle bracelet into the back seat.

"Earned my freedom?" Dan sputtered. "If she'd had a gun, she would have shot me! Why didn't you tell me you switched the pills?"

"Now, Son, did you really think I was going to give you another chance to run off with them?"

—⁓—

The transmitter under Edith's car had been picked up by unmarked cars on both sides of the bridge. She was heading north through Russellville on Hwy 7. The Sheriff, a deputy and Dan headed back that way too after they dropped Maezelle at her car. She agreed to meet them later then went back to pick up tapes and cameras and lock up. She was relieved that she had worn a thin pad to protect against sweat so no one need know about her personal experience behind the lilacs.

The red dot on the GPS tracker blinked on the Sheriff's console all the way through town and up to I-40. Surprisingly, Edith continued north past Dover and then west on 164 out toward the Piney. Then the dot disappeared. She had entered the area where cell service was sporadic at best.

"Damn," Deputy Dawson uttered, censoring his language for Maezelle's benefit. "She could be anywhere up there. How are we going to find her?"

"She'll come out some time, and we'll follow her then," Sheriff Wilson stated flatly. Things were not going as planned. They had fully expected the car to head back to Fayetteville.

The group listened to the tape and watched the digital images of Edith flinging the mucus-buster caplets onto the floor. She clearly knew that the drug was supposed to be packaged in capsules.

"Hmm, I wonder," the Sheriff thought out loud. "Maybe the bottle was for her all along. After all, Chet did hand them over to her out on the river. Still that little cooler had Jim's name all over it, so he must have been in on it too. I'm really not sure how all this works."

Edith carefully drove her big silver Buick down the muddy ruts to Jim's cabin on the Piney. She was still boiling mad when she hit the door. "That little bastard thought he was going to get away from me again," she fumed after she had explained the debacle to Jim.

"Look, Honey, you don't have to have that bottle. I've told you I have enough money for both of us. We can always get more stuff."

"No we can't," Edith sighed. "I still owe Chet for that bottle. I promised him I'd have the money tomorrow. I had a sale lined up later tonight."

"How much?"

"Two thousand."

"How much do you have on you?"

"Just $500," She lied.

"Tell you what, Sugar, I don't have enough on me, but I have a little in the safe at the apartment. What say we go back to my place? We can drive down in the morning and ole Chet will be none the wiser."

They closed up the cabin and headed back to Fayetteville leaving the GPS tracker to sit for another day.

—⚬—

When it became apparent that the tracking system was going to be slow in giving them new information, the Dallas three decided to return home to take care of their own badly neglected affairs. Party time was over for the time being. Time to pack it in for the day.

Maezelle called Sammy to get permission to leave the skunk for Dr. Frank. Then she packed up the rest of Sammy's surveillance equipment and brought it back to Garnet's. Colleen agreed to return the key to Janis at Sweet Home the next day. Meanwhile Maezelle called Janis and thanked her profusely in spite of the fact that she hadn't caught any ghostly behavior on her cameras.

—⚬—

The next morning, Dr. Norton was driving down the hill for his morning coffee and breakfast at Betty's

Café when he caught a flash of light on metal in his peripheral vision. Drat it! Johnny Earl and his cousin, Johnny Joe, known locally as the Johnny twins (more like Tweedle Dee and Tweedle Dum), were rabbit hunting on his property again! He had already chased them off any number of times making it very clear that the land was posted. There must be something really special about his rabbits to make them keep coming back.

He parked his Infiniti and walked down the path toward Mulberry Hall where he saw the two of them getting ready to blast the robo-skunk into the next century. "Wait, wait!" he yelled at them to distract them. "Don't shoot! That's my skunk!" He ran past them and grabbed the skunk reaching under it just in time to turn off the sprayer. Then he turned the skunk, tail first, toward the two who stood with eyes bulging and mouths dropping. "Now, which one of you wants to poach another one of my animals?" he demanded. The Johnny twins dropped the rabbit they had shot earlier and made a hasty retreat plowing through briars and poison ivy on their way to the truck. Not too long after, the rumors expanded. Not only was Mulberry Hall haunted with giant animals, but the whole property was guarded by rabid skunks!

21

Colleen was truly miserable the week following her arrest. She figured she had lost her Walmart job. The good news was that Sheriff McCurly had persuaded her manager to keep her. He hoped she'd recognize Chet since she usually cashiered in the evenings. The bad news was that she was on special probation and was constantly being monitored. She imagined that every customer who came through her line had seen her mug shot in the paper and judged her harshly.

By the second week, things were closer to normal. Colleen hadn't grown up in the area, and very few people knew her. If they remembered her it was because she was both cute and polite. With no effort on her part, she found an increasing number of young men queuing at her register. Some of them actually flirted with her, and she began to feel more like a human being.

She was caught completely by surprise one night when Dan Stapleton came through her line. "I need to talk to you," he said in a low voice so others couldn't hear.

"Well, I don't need to talk to you!" she muttered through partially closed teeth.

"Ah, come on, Colleen," he countered. "It's really important. When do you take your break?"

Colleen looked up to see the manager eyeing her. Cashiers were supposed to be friendly, but not carry on personal conversations, especially when their lines were backed up. "Not till 10:00," she offered smiling innocently for the manager's benefit.

"Meet me under the light at row thirteen," he insisted.

"Oh, very well," she agreed trying to get him out of her way.

When 10:00 came, she wavered, then decided she'd better nip this in the bud before she lost her job for real. She grabbed a drink and scooted out the automatic doors toward row thirteen.

Dan was sitting in an old beat-up pickup under the light. He motioned for her to get into the passenger's side. She climbed in reluctantly, glancing at her watch to drive in the point that she didn't have much time for this nonsense.

"I don't know what you want, but you'd better make it snappy. I have better things to do than waste time with you, you bastard!" she lit into him.

"Whoa, whoa," he held up his hands in mock defense. "I came to apologize to you. I've had some quiet time to think, and my Dad is right. I really screwed the pooch. And I dragged you into it. I never stopped to think someone might get hurt."

"No, you didn't," she was showing no mercy.

"I deserve to have you mad at me," he continued. "I just came to say goodbye. I'm not coming back to school this fall. Coach helped me find a job in Dallas. I'll be working at Cosmic Fitness as a manager and trainer. They'll pay me while I get my certification. I know it's not much, but it'll give me some time to get my head straightened out. I really am sorry, and I brought something that may help both of us. Here," he handed her a folded piece of paper.

"What's this?" she snorted contemptuously. "A love poem?"

"Yes and no," he was not going to be deterred by her anger. "It's not for you. It's for my family. Open it."

She unfolded the paper and saw a list of four names she could barely make out in the dim light.

"These are some of the guys I partied with. I know for a fact that they bought stuff from Hot Dog too. I figured if you gave it to McCurly, I could pretend that I didn't rat them out. I know it's cowardly, but I can't take another beating right now. I've been trying to stay off Hydrocodone (That's a joke, isn't it?), but I'm still pretty sore."

Colleen folded the paper and put it into her shirt pocket. She looked at her watch and opened her door. Then she reached over and gently patted his hand as she silently left him alone to wipe the tears from his cheeks.

—◊—

Colleen debated in her mind whether to give the list to Sheriff McCurly. Since she didn't know any of the four guys, she had no idea what she might be getting them into. What if she kept them from graduating or getting a good job? What if their families were penalized for their behavior? She had lots of what-ifs. Finally she went to talk to Aunt Garnet.

"Well, Sweetheart," Aunt Garnet counseled. "It's really a matter of priorities. On one hand you have a dealer who gave you some designer drugs that turned out worse than a snakebite. You nearly killed that boy with that marijuana. And, you know that this Hot Dog person is probably linked to whoever is selling designer Hydrocodone. We know that Hydrocodone is becoming very popular, especially among kids in your age group, and we know that sooner or later somebody overdoses and dies. On the other hand, you have the reputations of four young men who have been engaging in risky, illegal behavior that is increasingly being blown off. You've been arrested, and your life hasn't been ruined yet. Why are you so sure that their's will be? The choice is up to you, Hon."

Colleen continued to muddle over her dilemma. Ratting out someone you didn't even know for your own benefit just didn't seem right. The next morning while she was reading the local advice column she suddenly had an epiphany. There was a letter from a young teen:

Dear Missy,

I am 13 years old and have a huge problem. While my friend "Cleo" and I were at the department store, Cleo stole a really expensive pair of earrings. I told her she should take them back, but she said everyone does it, and it's no big deal. Should I say something to my parents? I hate to rat her out because I know I'll lose her as a friend. Please help me.

Scared to Tell

Dear Scared to Tell,

Yes you should tell someone. Shop lifting is stealing, and it is a serious crime. By keeping quiet, you make it easier for Cleo to do it again. Do you really want to hang out with friends who are in danger of being arrested? Don't try to handle this by yourself. Let an adult handle it for you.

Colleen felt more than a little embarrassed for herself. Here was a thirteen year old with the same problem essentially, and Colleen would have given the same advice. Yet, here she was worried about repercussions from "friends" she didn't even have, and the stakes were a lot higher than a pair of earrings. She called the Sheriff's office and made an appointment for a face-to-face.

Sheriff McCurly studied the list before asking the obvious, "Where did you get this?"

"Someone who came through my line gave it to me," she hedged, trying to protect Dan.

But the Sheriff had seen this before. He knew that young people were especially prone to feeling obligated to cover for friends with little white lies.

And adults were even worse. When a relative was involved it was true that blood was thicker than water. And it was also true that obstruction of justice was obstruction of justice no matter how well intended.

Curly looked her straight in the eye and asked her outright, "Was it Dan?"

"She ducked her chin just a little and breathed out a reluctant, "Yes."

Then the Sheriff said something that impressed her. "I'm real proud of that boy. He's done a lot of growing up this summer. He comes from good people, and I think he's finally coming to see that it's not all about him."

The list of four names proved to be a dead end, at least for the time being. Two of the guys had gone off to work on a fish factory boat in Alaska; one had gone home to Mississippi; and one was "just gone" for the summer. Sheriff McCurly was disappointed, but not discouraged. There'd be time enough to hunt these boys down later provided he was able to build a case.

22

Royce (Hot Dog) was not a happy camper. Both drop boxes at Clarksville had been empty this morning. The fallback was to wait 24 hours before making any contact just in case a delivery had been aborted for some reason. He'd be back tomorrow. It had happened once before, but he had a bad feeling about this.

Since he had a little extra time on his hands before his first house showing, he stopped at the Cracker Barrel at exit 81 off I-40 for some biscuits and gravy. He was perusing the local paper when he almost choked on his coffee. The State Highway Patrol had stopped a semi from Searcy and found a white powder believed to be cocaine. This was the second stop of couriers from Searcy this week. A young woman had been stopped almost 24 hours earlier carrying the same white powder to California.

Holy Shit! That's our stuff The State Patrol doesn't "just stop" people. They knew they were coming! I sure hope Brady got wind of this in time to clear out. I'd better see if our alternate is still up and running And, I'd better be damned careful.

The first call on his throw-away phone was to Chet. "Hey, Guy," he sounded cheerful, "did you see the Russellville paper? How about those Diamond Hogs? They've got a game tonight. Let's get together and watch it." Chet, Conner and Hot Dog talked in code regularly. Hot Dog knew Chet would alert Conner. They'd meet at "The Lodge" after dark tonight.

While Hot Dog was having his breakfast Drug Task Force and State authorities were serving a warrant on one, Brady Hines in Searcy, Arkansas. Based on information from the two mules who had been picked up outside Russellville, and the identification of Mr. Hines by a confidential informant, a judge had found probable cause for a search that interestingly had turned up 25 pairs of very expensive ladies shoes. However, Mr. Hines was nowhere to be found.

The meeting at The Lodge that evening was tense. Hot Dog was clearly agitated. His speech was staccato, and he kept tapping his heel on the concrete floor. "I can't believe they got all our shipment," he complained shaking his head in denial. "Somebody had to have tipped them off. But who? We've kept this thing so close there's no one in our group to point a finger at. Have either of you noticed anyone watching you a little too close?"

Both Chet and Conner denied any reason for alarm. Their pharmacy jobs were basically clean.

Most of the drugs came in from Mexico, and all the vials and labels came from a pharmacy supply company known for "private label" shipments to individuals. Even if the narcs had infiltrated that company, how would they know about Searcy? No, it had to be someone in Searcy.

Hot Dog reluctantly agreed and went on to the more pressing business of filling their existing orders. Chet and Dan had enough weed for the rest of the month and plenty of Demerol after the last shipment from Cameroon, but the Hydrocodone was running low. They'd been working on a new additive for the marijuana, and were playing with the idea of Demerol added there as well as to the Hydrocodone.

"OK, I'm on it," Hot Dog was thinking out loud. "I'll have to get The Big One to make a special contact for me. We should have something in a day or two. I'll let you know."

They left as they always did, a half hour apart. Hot Dog went through Dover, and the other two drove the back roads to Clarksville then to I-40. Chet got off at Exit 78, and Conner left the highway at Exit 81. They were all a little paranoid, but the trips back to Yell County went smoothly as usual.

The Big One acted with amazing speed, and Hot Dog was on his way to Fort Smith late the next morning. He stopped by Holiday Homes Realty to drop off some information for a customer who was considering buying a home for his son and his buddies while said son attended MNSU. His ulterior motive, of course, was to set up a believable alibi. Lunch with two of the realtors was an added bonus.

After lunch he made his way down Rogers to the west side of downtown turning north on Midland. He drove slowly looking for Big Jo's Antique and Flea market. He squeezed his car into an alley space and went inside. After he had browsed for a while, a rather buxom, overly made up, orange haired woman asked if he needed help finding anything in particular. "Well yes," he responded with the code, "I know this sounds silly, but I'm looking for something that would be suitable for a funeral urn for my mother's cat, Hairy."

"I'm so sorry," she offered "I love my cats, and when they die I have them cremated. I have quite a few urns on my mantel myself." She showed him several jars and vases, but none were just right. "I know," she exclaimed I have just the right thing for you! Wait here." She disappeared into the back and returned with a lovely cloisonné urn with a flat top. "Would this be satisfactory?" she asked as she slid back the lid to show him the cremains of an unidentified animal.

"Oh that's perfect!" he smiled. "It's just right for Hairy. What's your best price?"

"Well," she smiled through missing teeth, "Since it's for a cat, I can come down to, oh say, $50?"

He nodded his agreement and followed her to the cash register where she wrapped the urn in newspaper and put it into a used plastic bag. He paid her and left the shop after which she checked on her other customers' needs.

Whew! He thought to himself as he drove back across town and picked up 540, *That was really a trip. Even if I should get stopped, it's only an urn with burned bones. Great way to do it! The Big One sure knows how to set things up.*

He made one more stop about two miles up the Pig Trail from Ozark. One of The Big One's spies lived in a mobile home about an eighth of a mile off the road back from a line of six mailboxes. A middle aged man living on disability opened the door "Hey, Hot Dog, good to see you. That mother of yours isn't working you too hard in the real estate business, is she?" Bob Billings was an old family friend who knew Hot Dog's family from when he had lived in the Dardanelle area. He was also a seller of information about the drug trade in central Arkansas. "Heard Brady's mules got picked up. That's too bad. You manage to find what you needed in Fort Smith?"

Hot Dog nodded.

"Well, ole Brady's lit out for safer places. But he'll be back. He's got it sweet for Edith, ya know."

This was news to Hot Dog. Their rule was that the sales people stayed away from the suppliers.

"Oh, how so?" he asked to encourage Bob to go on.

"Well, it's just an observation on my part. She was over at Brady's a couple of weeks ago with that rich car dealer feller from Fayetteville makin' some kind of deal. But there was another deal goin' on under the table, if you know what I mean. He couldn't take his eyes off her."

"I didn't know ole Brady had it in him." Hot Dog mused "You just never can tell."

They jabbered for a while. Then Hot Dog got back on the road to Dardanelle. *The Big One is not going to like this,* he thought to himself. *Not only did Edith break the no contact with suppliers rule, but she took an outsider with her. Granted Jim had turned out to be a heavy user and a great customer, but rules are there to protect the operation. What is Edith trying to pull? Is she planning on going solo? Umm, Umm. Got to watch out!*

23

Things were still moving slowly for Colleen. She hardly knew what to do with herself when she wasn't at work. But when she was at work, she felt as if she were being watched all the time, especially by her manager. Then he cut her hours and put her on stocking from 10:00 pm to 4:00 am, just enough hours for the proverbial thirty-hour week.

She was stocking potato chips one night about 11:00 when a quiet voice asked, "When's your break?" She looked up to see Logan Tanner, the guy who had helped rescue her from the river party fiasco.

"Not until 12:00."

"Where can I meet you?"

"Outside. At the end of the cart return area." He didn't say anything else, so she spent the better part of an hour being paranoid. He was awfully cute with his dark curly hair and liquid brown eyes, but what could he want with her?

When she reached him, even in the dim light, she could see his crooked smile. "Whew," he said, "I was afraid you might not come."

"Well, I was almost afraid to come," she returned. "After our first (and last) meeting and everything that's happened since, I didn't expect I'd ever see you again."

"Nothing to be afraid of," he smiled again. "I just wanted to sit down and talk to you." He lifted his chin, and the subtle change in his mouth and eyes told her this was a male-female thing.

Now she smiled back shyly. "OK. I guess I can deal with that. But I've got to get back. I'm just on break now."

"When are you free for conversation?"

"I'm not off until 4:00."

"Then 4:00 it is. I'll see you then."

Colleen's mind strayed from her stocking several times during the next four hours. What had prompted him to come by? Was he as safe as he appeared? Did he have any ulterior motives? What if he wanted to ask her about drugs? Did he think she'd be easy since most of the local people were avoiding her?

True to his word, Logan was waiting for her at 4:00 am. They left her Mustang in the lot and drove his F-150 to the I-Hop on Highway 7 back in town. She couldn't help wondering if all the guys around here drove pickup trucks.

When they walked in, almost all the scattered customers looked up to inspect them. Logan waved at one of the tables, and everyone went back to business.

"Why is everyone so nosy?" she asked when they were seated.

"They don't mean anything by it," he soothed. "It's just a country way. Probably started when folks in small towns were suspicious of city slickers like you." He smiled to let her know he was teasing. "I bet you wouldn't see it at all at the I-Hop in Russellville where a lot of the customers don't know each other."

Logan ordered an enormous breakfast while Colleen stuck to easy to digest pancakes. Both drank coffee. While they waited for their order they began their conversation, one not dissimilar to others they'd had with other dates, except that the "getting to know you" ritual was a little easier because of their previous river meeting.

They found out that they were both seniors at UofA (small world). He was finishing in Animal Nutrition, and she, in Microbiology. He was from a cattle farm, and she was from the city, although her Grandpa (Mom and Aunt Garnet's Dad) had farmed in the River Valley, and her Uncle Add still owned a small farm north of London. They chatted for over an hour. Then he took her back to her car and asked if he could meet her at 4:00 am tomorrow.

Colleen wondered what he had seen in her to go to all the trouble to find her at Walmart. And she wondered how he was able to go without enough sleep to pick her up at 4:00 in the morning. The fact was that he had admired her spunk out on the river.

She had saved that lousy group a miserable night of critters and mosquito bites. And, besides, in his eyes she was one of the prettiest girls he had ever seen, well worth tracing back to her job in Dardanelle. The 4:00 routine was going to be a bit of a problem, though. He worked the river mostly on weekends to help out with the extra bookings and big parties. During the week he worked on his Dad's farm. It didn't take his Dad, Seth, long to figure out why he was staying out so late every night. But Seth just smiled and let Logan suffer from lack of sleep. Seth had been young once too.

Colleen's schedule jerked from early to late and back again throughout the summer. She was clearly just summer help, and the manager used her to his best advantage knowing she was unlikely to complain. It didn't matter. As long as his schedule allowed, Logan was there when she came off her shift no matter what the time. Through the summer they became inseparable. They had found the best place to make out. Colleen's Uncle Add had a big field with round hay bales off the road and out of site of his house. They'd take an old quilt out behind the rolls and spread it out. Then they'd lie there looking at the stars and making out. As the summer progressed, the dirt became drier and harder. Then Logan pulled some of the hay out of one of the rounds and made a softer love nest for them under the stars.

When they could get an afternoon off together, they usually headed for the river. Logan liked to go back to the gravel bar where they had first met. They were sitting on the gravel under a shade tree eating ham sandwiches and lazily watching the boats run up and down the river one day. "Wow," Colleen commented, "those boats are really fast. I wouldn't mind having one when I get some more money."

"You and me both," Logan countered. "I reckon I'll get me one when I win the lottery."

"The lottery? Just how expensive are they?"

"The boats aren't that bad. It's just the motors that go with them!" he laughed. "A big bass boat like that red one that just went by goes from $75,000 up, with a 500 HP motor."

"Oh, I had no idea," she mused. "They're all so pretty. I really liked the one Chet came in the day of the catastrophe. It was a dark glittery blue with baby blue chevrons all around the edge."

"There's only one of those on the river," Logan informed her. "That boat is really sweet. Belongs to Royce Haynes."

"Oh, I've seen him around, but I'm not sure I'd recognize him. He drives a black Lexus, doesn't he? They must be swimming in money."

"Yeah, I guess they own half of Dardanelle. They bought a lot of real estate through their agency. And when her husband died, folks said he left her $100,000 in insurance. Looks like she's invested pretty wisely. That Lizard Stop must be a gold mine. One of my old buds, Scott, works down there. He closes at night and clears the registers. They're doing right well. Funny thing, though. He said sometimes she forgets and leaves the deposit slips in the cash bag, and the slips sometimes show she deposited more money than they actually cashed out. I'm not sure how that works, but it sounds like a winner to me!"

24

After the three buddies went back to Dallas, things were quiet at the house. Colleen worked mostly nights and stayed mostly to herself except for an occasional date with Logan Tanner, the young man who had helped rescue the Fayetteville party from the river debacle. Garnet busied herself with getting all the beds changed, the bathrooms cleaned, and the refrigerator restocked.

Garnet kept her eye on the local paper. Since Colleen's arrest, she had become virtually obsessed with the local drug trade. There was an epidemic of arrests for possession of methamphetamine, but little attention to cocaine and prescription drugs. Surprisingly in one week there were two separate arrests of first a woman, then a man who were transporting cocaine across the state from, of all places, Searcy, Arkansas. The woman claimed she was being paid $2000 to transport the drug to California. The man, a trucker, was supposedly en route to Tuscon.

That doesn't make any sense, Garnet thought to herself. *Nobody transports drugs out of Searcy to*

California or Tuscon. They're going the wrong direction. There's something very weird going on. And how did they know to stop those two specifically? Then she remembered Rae's conversation with a friend who worked undercover drugs in the Dallas area. He said sometimes they knew who the mules were. Then they'd call ahead, sometimes to a different state if the haul was long, and the carrier would be picked up farther along the route. That way the carrier couldn't be sure who or where the dime had been dropped. *Someone was watching the pickups and maybe the drop offs!*

Then there was another strange story in the paper that week about a woman asleep on the ground in Veteran's Park. The article said that when she was found, she was in possession of a bag of prescription drugs. Evidently she had taken quite a few and was sleeping it off. The paper referred to her as "Sleeping Beauty".

Garnet called Hattie White at the crime lab and left a message. Hattie didn't call back until later that afternoon. She had been very busy testing and running down loose ends. The "cocaine" that had been confiscated was actually unpackaged Hydrocodone powder. The prescription drugs for "Sleeping Beauty" matched those from Dan Singleton's bottle. And, very importantly, the paper had not reported the fact that the meds were in a small red cooler just like the one Chet had delivered out on the river. And there were prescription bottles with the lady's name on them. They all checked out except for the bottle of Hydrocodone capsules. Her doctor hadn't prescribed it, and the pharmacy hadn't filled it. These designers were pretty slick. The pharmacy labels were dead ringers for the legitimate ones. Another thing that wasn't reported was that "Sleeping Beauty" talked in her sleep. She had kept mumbling sweet nothings to someone named Conner. That gave the investigators one more name to add to the puzzle.

—∽∽—

Garnet met some friends from work for lunch later that week then went to one of her favorite shopping places, Lyssia's Shoes in Dardanelle. Garnet was addicted to pretty shoes. Through the years, she had become friends with Alyssia Bergamont the owner. Alyssia had been widowed twice. The shoe store had been purchased with money from her second husband. Thanks to good taste and a head for business, Alyssia had saved a nice nest egg to be used when she decided what she wanted to do next. Now she was selling the store to begin law school at UofA

"Hi, Alyssia," Garnet greeted her friend. "How many more days now?"

"Garnet, Thank God you're here!" Alyssia turned the door sign to "Closed" and pulled Garnet into the back storage area.

"What's going on?"

"Look," Alyssia explained. "I just got this shipment of shoes from my Harlingen, Texas supplier. And there's something wrong."

"I don't see anything wrong," Garnet said as she opened several boxes of <u>Muniquitas</u>. "These are beautiful."

"I didn't order them! They're way out of our local price range even with the university crowd. And it's not just the shoes," Alyssia explained. "It's the drying packs." She pulled one out of a box and handed it to Garnet.

"I still don't see anything wrong," Garnet protested.

"I wouldn't have either if one of them hadn't split open. It's not drying compound. That's big chunky crystals. This is a very fine powder. I think it's dope. I'm so scared if it is, I'll be arrested. Me, who is going to go to law school, arrested for sneaking in dope in boxes of shoes!"

"Oh my," Garnet tried to think. "You have to call someone. Let me help. Since Colleen got mixed up with that Stapelton mess, I have the sheriffs of Pope and Yell County and the head of the Drug Task Force on speed dial. And I know a very good lawyer too!"

The Yell County Sheriff and a Drug Task Force agent came and took the shoes away, all 25 pair in their boxes. They questioned Alyssia carefully and asked her to come in later that afternoon to give them a statement. At no time did they reveal to her or Garnet that she had just provided an explanation for the 25 pairs of shoes they had found at Searcy. Plus, they now knew at least one of the ways drugs were coming into the area. And, if they could get either of the mules from Searcy to talk, they might find out who the drugs were intended for.

—◇—

That night Garnet emailed Mica with the fantastic story. Imagine! Sending drugs in shoes. Mica emailed back that the situation gave new meaning to "High" heels.

The next morning, Garnet was just getting ready to call Alyssia to see how she was doing and pass on Mica's pun when the phone rang. It was Alyssia.

"Garnet," she sounded hysterical. "I need help! Someone broke into the store last night and totally trashed it. Sheriff Wilson said they were probably looking for the drugs in the shoes! I'm so scared they'll come after me at home. He told me to cover up the windows then pack a few things and leave the house for a few days."

"OK," Garnet swung into motion. "I'll come down to help you. I have one of those packaging tools and a couple rolls of tape. Do you have something big to put over the windows?"

"Yes," Alyssia responded. "I have some big rolls of brown paper I was planning to use when I put everything on sale to liquidate. We can use those."

"You can come to stay with me for a while," Garnet soothed. "I doubt that anyone will look for you up here. Do you need me to pick up anything on the way down?"

"No. Just come quick. I feel as if I'm falling to pieces."

25

The Mt. Nebo Chicken Fry was an annual festival that started as a political rally where local politicians came to press the flesh and make emotional speeches about the certain demise of the State and the Arkansas way of life if the wrong party were elected. Then it evolved to a family festival with a big swimming pool and games for the kids. Next it became too big for the top of the mountain and was moved down to Riverside Park on Front Street in Dardanelle. Vendors' booths and games of "skill" soon followed. Now it was held at the Mt. Nebo State University True Grit football field with carnival rides and all the trimmings. The rainy day fallback was the giant Port of Dardanelle cafeteria just across campus.

Garnet was staying home because of the heat and the uncertainty of bathroom availablility. She was not particularly fond of porta-potties that would be there as backup for stadium plumbing. Besides she felt a strong need to stay close to Alyssia, who was not going anywhere close to Dardanelle, thank you. Colleen's new guy, Logan Tanner, who had helped rescue her from the disastrous river party, was out on the Arkansas on a party barge with a group from St. Louis. Colleen had been invited, but had sworn off river parties, at least for this year. So she went to the Chicken Fry with a couple of girls from work.

The three young ladies were glad the festival was on grass. Their trip through the crowded parking lot was like walking through a sticky sauna. The radiation from the asphalt was oppressively hot. As they made their way across to the main gate Colleen saw something that triggered a memory that disappeared in a flash. *I have no idea what that was about,* she thought to herself. *Oh well, better luck next time.* It couldn't be too important.

They decided to go on a ride before eating, considering the heat and the probable nausea factor, but they were discouraged by the price if the rides. The best buy, of course, was an armband, but that was out of the question. So they finally decided on the Ferris Wheel which they could all ride together. As they rose high enough to spot the blue Mustang on the parking lot, Colleen had the same microflash as earlier. Still, she just couldn't produce a clear memory.

After the Ferris Wheel, they stood in line for chicken and drinks and headed for the big tent with its tables and chairs and blessed shade. They were still sweltering in the heat and about to call it a day hoping they could find the elephant ears on the way out when Colleen saw something she did remember clearly. A few tables down two good looking guys were deep in conversation. Colleen was sure that one of them was Royce Haynes who had been at the real estate office when she had returned the Mulberry Hall key for Maezelle. The other man was none other than Chet, the man with the little cooler for Edith!

Colleen's first response was to stare, and she almost choked on a crumb from her biscuit. Then she got a hold of herself and looked away feigning interest in the little cutie at the next table. She used her phone to snap a couple of pictures of the little boy then cautiously snapped some of Chet and Royce. It was hard to get a full facial view of both of them, but she managed to fit them into the background of some shots of the other girls.

"Oh man, this heat is getting me," she complained. "I can't even eat all my chicken. Let's head back to the car. I think I saw a food truck with elephant ears back in that direction. I promised Aunt Garnet I'd bring her one." She pulled her ball cap even lower over her face and left the tent with the other two never looking back although she was tempted like Lot's wife.

When they were gingerly crossing the parking lot trying to minimize the amount of tar sticking to their soles, the flash of memory hit Colleen again. She closed her eyes and breathed slowly, trying to recreate the image that was swirling somewhere in her mind. It was that old Land Rover. Had she seen it somewhere? She didn't think so, but she knew her own thought patterns well enough to know that she wouldn't flash on an old Land Rover for no reason at all. So she took a picture. Then she took another including the license plate.

Colleen dropped her two friends off at the Walmart parking lot then hurried home. She could scarcely contain her excitement and burst through the door practically running. "Aunt Garnet," she exploded. "I've got him! I've got Chet!"

"Slow down," Garnet responded. "Just where do you have Chet?"

"I saw him at the chicken fry! I was so scared he'd see me, but he was talking to Royce Haynes from the realty office, and I don't think they ever saw me." She quickly flipped through the photos on her phone for Garnet to see.

"Oh my," Garnet showed her amazement. "Just email me all your photos from this afternoon, and I'll print them out."

When she finished printing the photos, she grabbed the artist's sketches for comparison and laid them out on the kitchen table. The sketch of Chet based on Colleen's description was actually a pretty good match.

"Now who is this, again?" Garnet pointed to Royce.

"Oh, that's Royce Haynes," Alyssia identified the young man. "His folks (or actually his mother; his dad is dead) own Sweet Home Realty, and he works for them. They have a really big business, and they're in Pope, Yell, and Logan counties. Mostly around Dardanelle and Russellville though. They're some of the 'in' people around here."

"Oh yes," Garnet remembered. "I called his mother, Janis, to help Maezelle set up her ghost finding equipment at Mulberry Hall."

"Oh, I see," Colleen interjected. "Logan told me the boat Chet was using that Saturday belongs to Royce Haynes. They must be good buddies."

Garnet continued looking at the photos and asked Colleen about the Land Rover.

"I'm not really sure," Colleen waffled. "I kept having some kind of memory flash. I know I've seen it somewhere recently, but I just can't place it."

"Well, it'll come back to you," Garnet trusted her niece's memory. "Meanwhile," she said as she checked her watch. "You'd better go ahead to work. I know you'd like to talk to the Sheriff, but they won't like it if you don't show up after being seen at the chicken festival."

After Colleen had gone, Garnet called Curly McCurly who said he'd be by to get a copy of the pictures later in the evening. Meanwhile Garnet and Alyssia continued to chat with the pictures still spread out on the table.

"I know I've seen this kid somewhere else," Garnet pointed to Royce Haynes. "But it could have been anywhere. If he's in real estate, he's probably all over the place. I've probably seen him when we were out to dinner sometime." She pulled the picture closer then looked at Alyssia. "I know who he is! Take a look at these." The anatomist in her surfaced as she aligned the second sketch with the picture. "Alyssia, meet Hot Dog! Seller of real estate and purveyor of drugs. This is the kid who sold marijuana to Colleen for Dan Stapleton!"

When Sheriff McCurly arrived, he was impressed with Colleen's and Garnet's detective work. He was familiar with both men. "Well, well," he mused, Chet Atkins and Hot Dog."

"Chet Atkins?"

"No. His real name is Chet Avery. But they call him Chet Atkins. He's a pharmacist at Living Well in Russellville, but he lives in Atkins. Bought an old Victorian house out there to renovate and drives a flashy red Corvette. Pharmacists can make a lot of money, especially if they work extra. He's not married so he probably picks up lots of weekends. Or, he picks up <u>and</u> delivers."

26

In the early afternoon while Garnet and Alyssia were taping up paper and packing clothes, Big Jo in Fort Smith got a call on her throw-away. "Get out today," the husky male voice instructed. "They've hit that shoe store in Dardanelle where the stuff was rerouted by mistake."

"OK," Jo agreed. "Sounds like it's coming down. I'll be out of town in two hours. Meet at the same place?"

"Yep. I'm on my way now. I'm takin' the Kansas route out. I figure they'll be lookin' for me on the northeast side of the state. You?"

"I'll go down through Oklahoma. I need to drop some stuff off along the way. I'll see you in a few days. Look for me when I get there."

Jo hastily gathered four funeral urns from the back of the store and placed them in the back of her Toyota. She closed the shop, took the money out of the till, turned off the lights and locked the door on her way out the back. She wasn't worried about fin-gerprints. They already had her prints, just not her identity.

At her small house she pulled into the garage and closed the double door. Quickly she switched the urns to the trunk of a large Chrysler with Texas plates. Then she hurried inside to pack her clothes and personal effects. When she returned to the garage, the frowsy redhead was gone. The woman who put her luggage into the big car seemed smaller, and her hair was a dirty blonde streaked with gray. She wore a conservative, tailored business suit with a soft white blouse, small opal earrings, and black shoes. She carried a large bag embellished with silver conchos, Texas style. She left the garish dresses and strappy sandals inside the house, but had packed the wild, red-head wig and the over-padded bras. No need to make it easy for them.

In two hours, as promised, she was across the Oklahoma border and headed for McAllester.

At McAllester, she had an early dinner at a Golden Corral then doubled back to the Memorial Gardens and Mausoleum on OK-69 coming south into town. She carried a duffle into the family section where she unlocked the door marked Sullivan. She deposited the four urns, took away some dried flowers and added fresh flowers to the crypt. She locked the door and patted it, a small nest egg safely tucked away.

Her stop in Sherman that night was quite restful. She had always had a bad feeling about that gang in Dardanelle and Russellville, so it was good to be shut of them. She stopped at Half Priced Books in Dallas to pick up some summer reading then headed to Houston. Another night on the road and she should make it to the valley.

After her night in Sherman, Texas, Jo's appearance was different. The navy suit and conservative shoes were gone, replaced with capris, an island shirt and flip-flops. Her hair was swept back into a clip except for a few strands around her face. But the night in Houston was truly transforming. She emerged in bright turquoise spandex topped by a flowing print with one shoulder bare. She wore black thongs with silver conchos and coordinating silver medallions in her ears. Her hair was a vibrant light auburn brushed back in layered waves. In short, she was hot!

Jo enjoyed the looks from handsome and not so handsome men. She had missed male attention during her stint as the frowsy Jo, but there was a whole retirement wrapped up in her celibacy. Besides, she had a special man waiting for her in the valley.

Secure in her disguise as herself, she enjoyed the long, but easy drive. First to Victoria where she stopped at the Faded Rose for a sandwich and a whopping order of fries and dropped off her suit at a local Good Will. Then to Refugio, Corpus Christi, and Kingsville. She was becoming road weary by the time she took the cut off at Harlingen and slowed for what seemed like perpetual road work all the way to Weslaco.

Jo turned north on International Blvd. and crossed through three lights before turning into the gated community of Snow Bird Hill. The name was humorous, not because of the "snow bird" designation, but because of "hill". The desert here was flat as far as the eye could see. The entire valley was dotted with tiny municipalities with never ending rows of mobile homes organized into fence-to-fence developments stretching to the edges of town. This was retirement Mecca. Housing and food were cheap, inexpensive restaurants abounded, state of the art medical care had followed the dollar to the valley, and cheap booze and medicines were just a ten mile drive away in Mexico!

She punched in the gate code and coasted through the rows of upper end double-wides. She smiled at the SUV in the drive. What luck. He was already here.

—⁓—

Brady had also undergone a transformation. He had dropped the beard, mustache and pregnancy puff before he left Searcy driving a Ford Focus with Kansas plates. Because of Harding University, local law enforcement was accustomed to out-of-state plates. He had headed across to Jonesboro to pick up Rte 55 north, staying away from Hwy 67. He thought he was a few hours ahead of the DEA thanks to a tip from The Big One that his mule had been picked up outside Russellville. He'd had that uneasy feeling lately, so he was packed and ready to go. His fool backup man had sent the truck driver out against Brady's advice. Oh well, more dope for the State Troopers.

He crossed back at Sikeston and drove all the way to Springfield where he spent the night. The next morning, a middle-class business man who needed his hair trimmed drove to Kansas City and crossed the bridge. He turned south and headed for Lawrence. Just outside the city, he stopped at a strip mall and went into a Fantastic Sam's for a short sports cut. Then he drove to a gigantic U-Store complex near the University of Kansas where he parked on the concrete street and opened a double-sized storage unit. He rolled his pilot's case inside and deposited it in the big, black Escalade with Texas plates. It took him a total of 10 minutes to make his last transformation. When he emerged he was wearing tight jeans with a silver bucking horse buckle and a blue and green western-cut shirt. He sported a thousand dollar pair of burnished cowboy boots, and to top it off, a three hundred dollar Stetson. What a hunk!

He left his old identity in a dusty duffle bag thrown carelessly onto a pile of old boxes. He then switched cars and emerged as a well heeled Texan heading south toward home.

He came down I-35 through Denton to Dallas then took the LBJ Expressway and headed out to Austin and San Antone. After a good night's rest in the Texas Hill Country, he drove to San Antonio then followed 281 to the valley where he cut back one last time to Weslaco. He slept in his own bed (one of many) and waited for Jo.

—⁓—

Jo and Brady, or Brooke and Don, or Baylee and Cody, or any number of aliases had been a couple for eight years. They were sometimes lovers and sometimes friends, but always partners. They moved to the same states together and located close enough to watch each other's back. They had dozens of disguises and had worked out elaborate codes for messages. Oddly enough, they didn't bank together or store their dope together. It just might have been a matter of trust.

"God, it's good to see you," Brady smiled. "But there's something different about you. Have you changed your hair? You know I liked it red."

She laughed at the private joke and gave him a big ole Texas kiss. "When did you get here?"

"Just last night. Seems like I drove half way across the country, but I reckon it's worth it."

"Yeah, I took a direct route, but I figured they were lookin' for you, not me. I could use a shower and a Margarita 'bout now. Care to join me?"

After they'd showered and made love, they sat at the little glass-topped table next to the window drinking Margaritas and munching on chips covered with melted cheese and jalapeno slices. The talk turned to business.

"What the hell's goin' on in Arkansas?" she asked.

"I don't have all the pieces, but I figure there's a rat in the mix."

"You mean somebody ratted us out? Who?"

"That's my best guess, but those guys up there are so screwy, it's hard to figure it out. The first I had an idea something was wrong, they picked up our carrier outside Russellville. I mean, what the hell? She was goin' the wrong direction for Christ sakes! It had to be a tip off. As soon as I heard, I got my ass out of there. Then that stupid Jerry sent out another package. Can you believe? Well I was almost to Sikeston by then, and you can bet your ass I kept going."

"So why did you call me?" she was still puzzled.

"Well, I checked in and The Big One said Hot Dog had made a buy from you to compensate. Then I got to thinkin', if someone was tryin' to shut Dardanelle down, then after Hot Dog's trip, they'd know about you too. So I called you."

"OK, she responded, "but I'm not sure anyone was on to me."

"Yeah, I know. But we didn't get here by being careless."

"So," she smiled at him. "Who's the rat?"

"Well," he answered slowly. "That's the problem. It could be that Chet guy, or it just might be Edith, or they could be in it together."

"How do you figure?"

"Well," he hesitated to gather his thoughts. "Remember the trouble started with that kid out on the river? Chet brings the stuff out to Edith, and the kid steals it. What if that was a set up? Now think about Chet. He's makin' big bucks as a designer. Why not take it all? And Edith. I swear that woman gives me the creeps. She showed up at my place with this rich car dealer, Jim. Said she needed a little bit to tide her over. She was all over me like ants on molasses. But she got real snitty when I told her I couldn't deal with her. Maybe she was tryin' to short-cut the buy. But my money's on her."

"Why?"

"Well, there's this woman down in Dardanelle that gets this load of shoes she says she didn't order. One of the dry packages is split open, and she get's suspicious and calls the police. The police take the whole shipment, shoes, dope and all. But that night, somebody breaks into her place and shreds it."

"So, somebody knew those shoes were coming," she surmised. He nodded his agreement. "But how do you find out who?"

"Well," he returned. "I think I got it figured out. Tomorrow you and me are goin' shoe shoppin'."

Brady went to retrieve still another throw away and dialed still another number. "Hey. Matt," he spoke to a man on the other end. "The lady is looking for some Muniquitas. You still stockin' them?" Jo listened to his end of the conversation. "Yeah, yeah, we're in town for just a few days.... OK.... What's a good time?... OK.... See you then."

"We're all set for tomorrow mornin' around 11:00. Think you can make it up by then?"

27

After a leisurely breakfast, Jo and Brady drove east to Harlingen for some shopping. Harlingen had a lazy downtown with small antique shops and a few boutiques. They strolled down the sidewalk, window shopping and picking things they wanted to look at later. Matthew's Fine Shoes had a lovely display of upscale shoes including a pair of Muniquitas that were to die for. They were in luck, the owner of the store, Matthew Ruiz, was in and waited on them personally. In between bringing boxes of the correct size and alternate selections, he chatted with Brady whom he referred to as Buddy. "Hey, Buddy, how long you here for?"

"Just a few days. Sissy here had to check on her <u>Granma</u>," he emphasized the word.

"Where you stayin' this time?"

"We're at the Best Western at Weslaco," Brady lied. "Thinkin' about crossing the border tomorrow. Is Prospecto safe, or has it turned into a drug war like the others?"

"Oh, I think you can cross there without much worry, but I wouldn't stay too long. Just buy what you need then come back. You never know who's watching you; so you have to watch your own back."

"How early do we have to go to get parking?"

"Oh, I think if you get there between, say, 9 to 9:30 you'll be OK. I always park down by the Canada store. There are parkers there that keep a watch on your ride."

Brady nodded his understanding and turned to Jo. "You picked out some shoes, Baby?"

"You bet!" Jo never missed a chance to pick up more Muniquitas. "I've actually picked out two pair." She handed her choices to Matthew who took them to the counter for Brady to pay for. Unfortunately, he'd want some form of pay back later.

As they left the shop, Brady turned and asked, "What's a good spot for lunch?"

"Oh, try Alfonso's. Their shrimp diablo are the best in the valley!"

The partners lunched and shopped and went back to Snow Bird Hill to wait for another day. They'd meet Matt tomorrow between 9 and 9:30 at the Canada store across the border.

—⚏—

They got up early enough for a quick breakfast with just one cup of coffee. Restrooms could be a problem for shoppers in Prospecto. They dressed plainly so as not to attract attention. Brady's SUV would make the short trip. They could see better out of it, and the dark tint on the windows would make them harder to see from the outside.

There was a short que at the bridge over the Rio Grande going south in comparison with a line of trucks that backed up two blocks waiting to be allowed to cross into the USA. The armed policeman was waving passenger cars through to the Duty Free Zone, but stopped at Brady. The officer motioned for Brady to pull over into an oblique parking lane near other vehicles that had been stopped. Brady and Jo were asked in broken English to get out of the SUV. They stood to the side watching the team of men with rifles over their shoulders go through the vehicle as if they were looking for large grains of sand. Smuggling went both ways these days: guns in; drugs out.

"What are they looking for?" Jo asked with alarm in her voice. She stared questioningly at Brady, asking him silently if he had anything to hide. He didn't. Still the whole scene made him very nervous, especially since there was a high probability it would be repeated on the way out.

They were being allowed to climb back into the SUV when the rifles came up, and their hearts stopped. Jo sucked in a large and noisy breath. But the rifles were not for them. They were for the car two slots away where a huge commotion began. A rifle had been found wired to the muffler, and the car was being tipped over to reveal its belly. They couldn't see the face of the doomed driver who was being dragged off by three officers.

"Whew," Brady sighed his relief as he passed through the Duty Free Zone and headed toward the Canada store. "I'm just glad we weren't driving one of those Stow-and-Go things. Can you imagine?"

Luckily, there were still a few parking places, and Brady let his parker guide him into a spot. He checked his Citizen and exhaled another sigh of relief. They had five minutes to spare. When they entered the store, they split up. Jo went to the pharmacy to pick up antibiotics and Retin-A while Brady browsed in the garden decorations. He was admiring a large emerald frog emblazoned with orange and cobalt flowers, when he heard Matt's voice.

"Hey, Buddy, it's good to see you," Matt said loudly and held out his hand.

"Chris Gonzales," Brady picked up the subter-fuge. "How long has it been?"

"You need to buy shoes?" Matt asked in a soft voice.

"How are Margarita and the kids?" Brady asked loudly then dropped his voice. "No, but I need to know who did. The Dardanelle buy?"

"Oh, they're great. Kids growing up too fast you know. How's your Edith?"

"Oh, she's fine too," he nodded his understanding. "She's over in the pharmacy buying face creams. Always trying to look young, you know. Are you still taking care of your *mother in Mexico*?"

They slapped each other on the back and made chit chat about getting together soon. Then Matt had to run to get back to Harlingen for lunch, and Brady went to look for Jo.

The trip back across was thankfully easy. They propped their few purchases on the dashboard for ready examination, denied purchasing any pro-hibited antibiotics, displayed their passports, and drove back into Texas.

Later that night, Brady made a terse phone call. When the phone picked up, he uttered only one word, "Edith."

28

Later that evening, Hot Dog received a cryptic call. "You boys better go fishing for a while. Things are starting to heat up. Contact the usual way."

Hot Dog immediately called Chet and Conner. They agreed to meet at Hot Dog's at 6:00 the next morning. They would take hunting and fishing equipment including a tent, clothes for a week, and, of course, their burn phones. They'd pick up a few groceries along the way. Hot Dog made a quick trip to Walmart to pick up enough frozen entrees, etc. to fill a freezer chest.

The next morning, they met as planned and transferred everything into Conner's old Range Rover. The Lexus and the Corvette were too fancy and too low to the ground for where they were headed.

They followed AR-22 to New Blaine then turned south to Danville then picked up AR-27 following it to AR-28 to SH-307 near the Fourche River inside the National Forest. They drove very slowly as Hot Dog consulted an old hand-drawn map. "There. There." He indicated a narrow, grown over lane that angled sharply up a bluff. Conner shifted down and started the climb. As they bounced over deep ruts, the bushes scraped and rattled against the side of the Land Rover making Conner wonder if he'd have any paint left.

When they reached the giant tree that had been deliberately felled across the road to keep trespassers out, Conner parked the Rover on the little turnaround. "It's all packing from here on in," Hot Dog explained. "But let's cover the Rover before we leave."

They used the camouflage tent to cover the vehicle then picked up as much personal stuff as they could carry. They'd come back for the cooler later. The hike was mercifully short. About a quarter mile up the path they approached an old single-wide mobile home that had been brought in years ago when the road was still passable. The owners had used it as a camp for hunting and fishing. One of Hot Dog's uncles had bought it later, and he had left it to his sister, Hot Dog's mother, when he died. It would be a long time before anyone found them here.

29

Jim Strothers' soon to be ex wife, Jeanine was in a snit. *That goddamn Jim! Why can't I ever get a hold of him?*

Jeanine walked from the study cum office into the kitchen to get a beer, something to calm her nerves. She knew he was out there with that Edith person, but he wouldn't answer his phone. *Probably in his little love nest down by Dover. Sure there isn't any phone service, but what kind of excuse is that? They had to go out sometime, don't they? He's still in touch with the dealership according to Mary in the office. He just can't make it easy can he?*

By the time her companion, Pat, came home from the bank, Jeanine had chugged two more beers and was past whiny all the way to belligerent. Pat knew the drill by now and was getting a little whiny herself.

"Come on, Jeanine," Pat tried to reason with the woman who was slinging dishes into the sink. "Sure he's a jerk, but it's almost over. If he want's to dick around awhile, it's no skin off your nose."

"I know," Jeanine admitted. "But it's so unfair. I'm up here trying to get all this property settled and he's down there smoking dope and carrying on with that Edith woman! It wouldn't hurt him to come up here and sign a couple of goddamn papers for me! After all, I have a life to live too."

This from the woman who was suicidal six months ago. Pat thought.

It HAD been tough on Jeanine. It wasn't Jim's philandering though; he'd always had a roving eye. Jeanine had been one of those flings early in the game. She knew what he was, but she wanted his life style. It took a while for the gold digger to realize that all that glitters is not gold. Still, they had kept up appearances. And Jeanine wasn't above a little something on the side herself although her taste turned to women.

It had all started unraveling when she was diagnosed with breast cancer. She was devastated, but Jim seemed indifferent and became busier than ever "at the office". She didn't know how she would have made it through the mastectomy and chemo without Pat.

Then her hair fell out! That was the last straw for Jim who refused to be seen with a "hairless dog with only one boob."

She had filed for divorce. Jim had moved out into one of several of his little love nests. Pat had moved in to nurse Jeanine. And the rest was still in progress.

"OK, what is so important that Mr. Jim has to sign right away?" Pat asked.

"It's the property settlement we agreed on. It has to be signed so it can be filed with the court."

"When?"

"Yesterday. No kidding. I've been trying to reach him for two days. His lawyer wants to renegotiate (more money for him). If we don't get this in by tomorrow at the latest, we may have to do the property settlement all over."

"Or, you could just shoot him," Pat joked. "Then you could have it all."

"Believe me. I've been tempted, but no thanks. That bastard isn't worth a bullet."

"So what are you going to do?" Pat asked.

Jeanine paused for emphasis, "I am going to get up in the wee hours and drive down there to catch the slimy little piss-ant and 'Lady Edith' so early they can't get away from me. I am going to get that signature if it kills him!"

30

Around 7:30 am the next morning, the big red car sloshed through the mud puddles and ruts moving slowly to avoid scraping the bottom out. The driver pretzeled out and strode toward the front door of Jim's cabin. Jim and Edith were still asleep in the bedroom when the driver pushed the unlocked door open and entered the tiny front room. They were startled from their sleep as the bedroom door crashed against the wall.

"What the hell?" Jim questioned then shut his mouth. He was looking at the Colt-45 pointed straight at him.

"What do you want?" Edith demanded, seemingly oblivious to the danger at hand.

"I only want what's fair," the driver stated flatly. "You, you bitch," the gun swung toward Edith. "That order of shoes in Dardanelle. You were greedy and stupid. Did you really think I wouldn't know you were trying to cut in on my business?"

Before Edith could protest with lying denial, the gun turned back toward Jim. "And you, you cost us the whole Searcy load, you despicable snitch, or should I say, 'CI'?"

Edith's eyes widened as she looked at Jim and sputtered, unable to take it all in.

"Oh, yes," the driver snarled. "You two are a fine pair. I couldn't figure out who had tipped off the Task Force about the Searcy drops. Then Bob Billings told me you had been together at Brady's. You both screwed me. Now it's my turn," the driver smiled as two bullets were fired, then two more.

The driver hurried to the car and retraced the road with a slight detour to hide the gun for later use. The car turned onto the big gravel road and picked up speed almost running over a Park Ranger who was standing in the middle of the road yelling, "Left of center! Left of Center!"

The big car reached the Y in the road and slid around the corner toward The Lodge. Pulling up into the front yard, the driver jumped out of the car and grabbed a can of gasoline from the back. The back door opened easily with the key. A knowing push and the stairs to the basement were revealed. Gasoline splashed all over. A match. The damage was done.

The driver ran to the car being careful to stay on the grass. Footprints in the mud would be too telling. Once again the car reached the Y. Then it roared down the road toward the Twin Bridges and pavement.

There was one more stop on the road toward Russellville and Dardanelle. The car was covered with mud! There was a new U-Pump just north of the bridge over the Illinois after the HWY-7 bypass west of Dover reentered the main highway. The driver stayed on the outside of the pumps farther from the cashier and paid for a car wash with a prepaid credit card, then picked up the bypass and cruised back toward town.

—w—

Jeanine hated early mornings, but she wasn't about to renegotiate the settlement with Jim and his dip-shit lawyer always drooling at the mouth. She stopped in Clarksville and took the scenic 164 route toward the Twin Bridges. The strong coffee plus the sugar from a sticky doughnut helped keep her awake on the narrow, sometimes curvy, road.

She hated the gravel and mud roads out to the cabin. She hadn't been there herself for several years, so it wasn't surprising that she missed a turn and had to back up. Truth be told, she was so immersed in her inner ranting that she wasn't paying good attention and almost got the Mercedes completely bogged down in a mud hole.

By the time she got to the cabin, she had managed to work herself up again and was loaded for bear (or bare; whichever). She bounded up the steps, pushed the already opened door aside and stomped into the room. The stomping stopped and the screaming began. If there had been any neighbors, they would have heard her. Jim and

Edith were both crumpled onto the bed with parts of their faces missing, and there was blood. Blood everywhere.

—⁓—

Olivia Hubbard had been checking on her emus and was walking slowly back to the shade of the porch when she heard a vehicle traveling fast down the gravel road toward Twin Bridges. She looked over her shoulder in time to see a red blur pass by. *My, my, he's certainly in a hurry. Hope he doesn't run over any wild turkeys down by the creek.*

Not more than three minutes later another car came roaring down the road. To Olivia's surprise, it turned into her driveway and flew toward the house flinging rocks and kicking up choking dust along the way.

"Quick! Quick! Do you have a land line?" the nearly hysterical woman tumbled out of the silver Mercedes and ran toward Olivia who nodded her yes.

"Call 911! I think they're dead! They've been shot!"

Olivia ushered the distraught woman into the house toward the phone trying to get more information as they ran. "Slow down just a little bit. Who got shot? Where?"

"Jim and Edith," the woman stammered. "They're in his cabin over on the Piney."

"Where on the Piney? You know these roads are a mess. Can you draw me a map?"

The woman nodded, and Olivia stuck a pencil and paper from the phone table under her nose while she dialed the phone. She gave the emergency dispatcher detailed directions to the house and tried to make sense of the woman's map, but couldn't.

"Very well," the 911 dispatcher instructed. "Emergency vehicles are on the way. Please stay where you are until they arrive." After verifying her phone number for the third time, Olivia hung up and turned to see the woman dashing out the door toward the Mercedes.

"Wait!" she shouted catching up with the woman and grabbing her arm to stop her. "You have to stay here until the police get here."

"No, no," the woman countered. " I have to get back to see if I can do anything!" She jerked her arm free.

"No you don't," Olivia countered grabbing both arms this time. "You have to be here to show them the way to the cabin! I can't read your map! They'll need you."

When the first car arrived from the Dover Police, the officer found the two women sitting on the porch steps. He recognized Olivia. She had her arm around the other woman trying to comfort her. Olivia quickly rushed the woman to the car before the officer could get out. "Here," she pushed the woman into the now unlocked front passenger seat. "You show him where to go; he'll let the others know."

Just then Olivia saw something that struck fear into her soul. Smoke! Fire in the woods! As she stood paralyzed, a thick black cloud billowed up on the west side of the Y. Carbon! Probably from a roof. How many houses were on that side of the road? As she tore toward the house to make her second 911 call of the day her thoughts rushed with her. *If it comes this way, I've got to save the emus! The road makes a fire break, but is it wide enough?*

The 911 dispatcher was surprised to hear from Olivia again, but remained calm even though Olivia didn't. "There's a fire over on the west side of the Y just past my house! I think it's the old Anderson house. Take the third right past the west branch at the Y then turn hard left at the big curve. It's back in there somewhere!"

All the volunteer fire departments in the area responded. After about 15 minutes and several quarts of adrenalin, Olivia saw a dusty parade of fire engines barreling down the gravel road and heard them head west. Only then did she start to relax, and then to shake.

31

The aftermath of the murder and arson was chaotic, to say the least. Sheriff McCurly set up a command post at Olivia's and began the convoluted process of sorting crimes. After the Coroner had removed the bodies and the Fire Chief had verified arson, trained investigators began the arduous process of reconstructing the two crimes.

Jeanine's stated time of arrival at about 7:30 and Olivia's sighting of smoke shortly after 8:00 helped nail down the time line. To rule out Jeanine's possibly having shot Jim and Edith then pretending to have found the bodies, her hands were bagged and her clothes confiscated for gunshot residue tests. The inside of her car was also swabbed. She had a concealed carry permit, but her gun hadn't been fired.

Interestingly, the outside door knob of the cabin had been wiped clean (Jeanine had stated that the door was open when she arrived.). And there were no shell casings in the bedroom. The killer had either worn gloves or wiped the door knob clean. If gloves could be found, they could be tested for gunshot residue and maybe finger prints. But the probability was quite slim. The murderer had not taken the plentiful pills from the lamp table by Edith's side of the bed. It appeared that drugs (at least not these drugs) were not the motive.

There were tire tracks all over the yard and driveway to the cabin, including quite a few from the various investigators. The first responders had failed to secure a reasonable perimeter, and any evidence had literally been run over by a car. However, the turn-off just past the cabin was clearly of interest. The investigators found two sets of different tracks there. Jeanine described, on further questioning, missing the turnoff then backing in to the next drive to turn around. One set of tracks confirmed her story. But the second set was puzzling. This vehicle had driven through the puddles and mud about an eighth of a mile before turning around at an old abandoned home place. What? Why? Who knew?

Tire tracks back to the Y in the road had been rolled over by too many vehicles. And the tracks back to The Lodge were a squished mishmash. However, the fire fighting crew had saved some of the tracks near the front of the house. And these matched the ones that had driven up to the old home place near Jim's cabin. It appeared that the murderer had struck Jim and Edith first then set the fire at The Lodge. And, it was quite likely that the culprit was driving the red car that had flashed past Olivia's earlier this morning.

Although the fire had done plenty of damage, it had traveled upward toward more oxygen, and a lot of the basement was salvageable. Remnants of a drug lab were still identifiable, including melted bottles of a powder that tested as Hydrocodone and several scorched bundles of marijuana. A refrigerator full of various prescription drugs was virtually undamaged. The arsonist had failed to destroy the evidence of a designer lab.

Before closing up shop at Olivia's early in the evening, Sheriff McCurly was surprised by a visit from Ranger Tidwell who almost had smoke blowing out his ears. "I heard you had a murder over on the Piney this morning," he said almost as an accusation. "Well, I want you to know I almost got run over this morning, and that would've been murder too!"

"Whoa, whoa," Sheriff McCurly tried to slow him down. "When was this, and where?"

"It was on the Forest Service road east of the Y. First thing this morning. This big red Corvette came roaring down the road over the speed limit and left of center! I tried to flag it down, but it just kept coming. I had to jump into the ditch to keep from getting run over!"

"And you're just now telling us?" The Sheriff was incredulous.

"Well, there was lot's of traffic today, and I had to make sure nobody got hurt on government property," he said as if that explained everything.

"Did you see who was driving?"

"Nah, it all happened too fast. But it had to be some crazy woman. You know what kind of drivers they are."

The Sheriff ignored that last statement and assured the ranger he'd put the incident in his report. When the ranger was gone the Sheriff sat for a few minutes just shaking his head.

The Ranger's story was a bit of luck that confirmed police work from earlier in the day. A search for the red car had, of necessity, taken opposite directions: one toward Clarksville, and one back toward AR-7. At AR-7 the officer elected to turn south. Since it was likely the entire drug operation was local, better to check close by then expand the search as needed. As it turned out, the officer got lucky. He stopped at the U-Pump just north of the bridge over the Illinois not far from the 7-Bypass west of Dover. The attendant remembered a very muddy Corvette that had fueled and gone through the carwash about 8:00 that morning. No, he hadn't seen the driver who had paid at one of the outermost pumps. Yes there would be a record of the transaction. No he didn't see which way the Vette went.

The red Corvette, the designer lab, Colleen's picture of Chet and Hotdog, Chet's PharmD, all pointed to Chet, although a motive for murder wasn't at all clear. The Sheriff had one of his men check at the Be Well Pharmacy where Chet was known to work. Chet hadn't come in today. He had called early to say he was going fishing so the pharmacy could get a substitute. The next check was at Chet's house in Atkins, but he and his Vette were gone.

Finally Sheriff McCurly and a homicide detective from Yell County drove over to Hot Dog's place out on the river. They knew from Colleen's Chicken Fry pics that the men were working together in the local designer trade. There in the driveway were a Lexus and a red Vette. A cursory examination of the big rear tires showed a good match for the tracks near the murder scene and The Lodge. But the tires were mostly clean, and unfortunately, the law officers didn't have a warrant. The detective called his dispatcher to enlist the desk sergeant to begin the process. They had just climbed back into the car when a big red Cadillac rolled up the front drive and Janis Haynes got out.

"Officers," she greeted them tentatively. "Is there a problem?"

"We're not sure," the detective explained. "We were hoping to talk to Chet Evans about a pharmacy matter."

"Oh my," she offered. "Has there been trouble at Be Well ?"

"No, Ma'am." We just needed to check on his whereabouts. A red Vette was seen near one of our crime scenes earlier today. Just routine police work."

"Well, I can't believe Chet would be involved in anything criminal. He's good people. He and my son, Royce and another pharmacist (I think his name is Conner.) left this morning for a week's fishing trip."

Sheriff McCurly pulled out his note pad. "About what time did they leave this morning, Mrs. Haynes?"

"I'm not really sure. They were still waiting for Chet when I left for the office at about 8:30."

"Do you know where they were going?"

"No. But I'm assuming Bull Shoals. Royce loves to fish up there. He says he always catches fish at Bull Shoals. He's been going there since he was a boy. My late husband used to take him every year. You know, just father and son time," she chattered on.

"Do you know what vehicle they went in?"

"Yes," she laughed. "That Conner, or whatever his name is, was driving an old Range Rover. You don't see very many of those around here. Lots of old Mercedes, but not so many Rovers. I remember when all the University crowd started buying up old diesel Mercedes because they were supposed to be better for the environment. You couldn't prove it by me, not with that horrible smelling smoke. I always say, 'Give me a good American car. They're still the best buy for the money'."

"Color?" he asked, looking down to write on his pad being careful not to encourage her.

"Now, let me think. It was an off white with something close to maroon, or maybe red, trim. You know how these old cars are. The colors fade after so many years."

They thanked her and asked her to let Chet know they wanted to talk to him if the fishing party happened to call in. Then they drove back to Dardanelle and issued a BOLO for a white Range Rover with red or maroon trim anywhere in the north part of the state.

Something else about the Range Rover kept tickling the Sheriff's memory, but he just couldn't pull it out. Then he remembered. Garnet's niece had taken a picture of a Range Rover at the Chicken Fry thinking the pic might be useful, but not really knowing why. And Garnet thought she had seen the Rover someplace too. He called Garnet, but she still couldn't place the vehicle.

—◊◊◊—

When Colleen came in from work the next morning, Garnet asked her about the pic. "I know this sounds silly," Colleen mused. "But it's associated in my brain with emus. And I've never been out to the emu farm."

Emus! Of course! Valentine had taken pictures at the house where she and Mazelle had found the emus. She grabbed her phone and called Valentine who was just leaving for work in Texas. "Hey, Sis," Garnet started. "We need your help again. Do you still have those pics of the house where you found the emus on your phone?"

"I'm not sure. Here, let me take a look. Yep got 'em. Why?"

"We're looking for any pics with an old Range Rover in them. I think I remember seeing a Rover off to one side, maybe under a shed or something."

"Oh, yeah," Valentine responded. "There is one, and here's another one. You really do have a good memory. I'd forgotten all about that."

"Unfortunately, it wasn't my memory. It was Colleen's. And she wasn't even there."

"Well, why d'yall need it?"

Garnet filled her in on yesterday's events including the situation with the Range Rover the three men had taken, one of them being a suspected murderer. "If your pics and Colleen's are a match, then we have the license plate too! It'll make the BOLO much more effective."

"OK. I'll email these to your computer so you can print them out. Son of a gun! This is exciting. I've got to run. I'll be late as it is. But this is worth it. Call me at work in about half an hour. I can't believe I may actually have some important evidence!"

Garnet printed out Valentine's pictures while Colleen retrieved their suspects folder from the file cabinet. The Rover was quite small and slightly unfocused in the two pictures, but a close comparison showed a match. Garnet reached for the phone and called the Sheriff. He wasn't in, but the sergeant promised to contact him immediately and to update the BOLO as soon as he got the go ahead.

The license plate number was indeed helpful. It led to a name, Conner Drummond, and an address in Dardanelle. Conner's neighbors were the neighborly type. They knew that he was a pharmacist who worked at Harlan's Pharmacy. They confirmed that he drove an old Range Rover and that he had a friend who drove a red Corvette.

Sheriff McCurly was relieved that one more piece of the puzzle was falling into place. They now had the Rover at the drug house. And they had two pharmacists who were up to their necks in felony manufacture of drugs. Colleen's two pictures of the Rover were included with the names of the three men in the updated BOLO.

32

By the third day of their adventure, Chet, Conner and Hot Dog were beginning to get stir crazy. They were about three quarters of a mile over very rough terrain from the Fourche River and good fishing. But they figured they'd better walk in case someone was looking for the Rover. By the time they made it to the river and back, they were hot, sweaty and ill tempered. All the beer was gone, and the well was marginal, so long showers were out of the question.

The worst part was the not knowing. Not knowing what was going on at home; not knowing how long they needed to stay in hiding; not knowing if they even needed to be hiding, etc. They finally agreed that since Hot Dog had the best "ears on the ground" in Dardanelle since his mother knew everybody in town, he should take the Rover and drive back toward Lake Nimrod until he could get a phone signal because there certainly wasn't one around here.

Hot Dog had to drive half way between Rover and Plainview before he got a signal. He pulled off behind some trees to make the call to The Big

One. He kept getting voice mail, so he waited impatiently, calling again every fifteen minutes. After about an hour, the phone was finally answered.

"Sorry to keep you waiting, but I was with a client," The Big One explained curtly. "There's real trouble here. Someone shot and killed Edith and her friend, Jim, yesterday. Sheriff McCurly in Russellville is looking at Chet." The information continued in spite of Hot Dog's indrawn breath. "There's a BOLO out for all three of you for Felony manufacture and distribution. In short, get the hell out of Dodge!" The phone went dead. Not enough time for any tower triangulation (not three towers anyway).

Hot Dog sat silently in the Rover, stunned. *Shot to death? Why?* Then he remembered Bob Billings' telling him that Edith had been at Brady's around the time the Searcy mules had been arrested. *Edith selling them out? Nah, couldn't be. But then she could be a real bitch. Still...*

Hot Dog took a gamble and drove all the way into Plainview where he gassed up and bought food bars and bottled water. They'd have to lie low the rest of the day and start out about dark. He figured Dallas was their best bet, but they'd have to huddle on that decision.

The other two were clearly rattled by Hot Dog's news. They wanted to leave immediately, but Hot Dog talked some sense into them. They discussed doubling back to the Fourche Mtn. Camp Grounds to try to steal a car, but decided against it. No doubt the police or Sheriff from Yell County would have talked to Hot Dog's Mom, so they would know they were in the Rover. But Hot Dog's Mom would have sent them to Bull Shoals because that's where they usually went. So they could probably get out of Arkansas before the law caught on. And stealing a car would call attention, sure thing. The nearest airport of any size was Fort Smith, but it was too risky. It was Dallas or bust.

The plan was simple. They would stick to back roads until they made it to I-30. Then they'd shoot into Dallas and Grape Vine. They'd leave the Rover in remote parking where it was unlikely to be found for several days. Chet would fly to Acapulco where he had a time share. It was really important that he get out of the country. Hot Dog and Conner could figure out where they wanted to go as they drove west.

It was a good thing they didn't have many clothes. The washer took almost an hour to fill from the marginal well. They pooled laundry into two loads, not worrying too much about separating lights and darks.

Then they repacked their backpacks. They took their fishing equipment as part of their cover, and Chet insisted on taking his rifle. If they got split up, they'd keep on going and all head to Mexico as soon as possible.

As twilight fell, they loaded quietly into the Rover, subdued by the enormity of their task. They picked up 307 and headed west toward the Forche

River bridge. They'd pick up 28, then 71 to De Queen. They were approaching the river, moving at about 55 mph, when a deer jumped out of nowhere and tried to clear the hood. Conner swerved sharply to the left and hit the rocky bluff bordering the road. Then he overcorrected and ran off the shoulder on the right. He saw the small bolder just a second too late. He swerved again, but the right tire hit it with full impact, and the Rover began to slide then rolled down the steep bank toward the river.

Mercifully the Rover landed upright with a bone-cracking jolt on a little gravel bar just shy of the water. They had all three been wearing seat belts just to help stabilize them in their seats on the twisting road, but they were not all right. Conner had hit the steering wheel with his chin, and he had run his right foot all the way through the floor board. At the present, he was out cold. Hot Dog had numerous bumps and bruises and could hardly breath because of cracked or broken ribs. Only Chet seemed to be unscathed except for a deep bruise across his abdomen from the seat belt.

The bank was too steep for Hot Dog to navigate, so Chet opened up the emergency pack and climbed up the bank to set flares. Then he changed shoes and retrieved his back pack and his gun. They said a quick goodbye, and Chet crawled back up the bank, stepped over the dead deer, and vanished into what was now night.

33

It was a half hour that seemed as if it were a year before Hot Dog heard a car on the road. He struggled to climb the steep bank on his hands and knees gasping for breath and agonizing every time he took one. The flairs that Chet had set should stop the driver, but he was afraid of being passed by since the Rover was off the road and out of sight. He crawled upward toward the edge of the bluff too late to attract attention. But he needn't have worried; the dead deer in the middle of the road did the trick.

Harvey Tuttle had to stop because he couldn't get around the doe on either side. He was tugging on her hind legs and muttering to himself when Hot Dog scared the living daylights out of him with his moaning, "Help us." He let go of the doe and the recoil from his pulling propelled him backwards until he almost stomped on Hot Dog's hands.

"Land of Goshen!" He screeched. "I thought you was long gone! What in tarnation are you a doin' out here?" He was certain that he was seeing the ghost of his cousin who had died of liver cancer three years past.

"Down the bank," Hot Dog moaned. "Car wreck. Friend hurt bad. Please help."

Harvey slapped his hand over his bearded mouth and rolled his eyes until they almost went back into their orbits. "Well I'll be a son of a skunk. You ain't cousin Willis." He sighed with relief. "How'd you get down there, Mister?"

Hot Dog was not in shape for long explanations. He pointed to the deer, then down to the river. "Friend hurt bad," he managed between clenched teeth.

"Well, Mister, you don't look too good neither," Harvey answered him. "Let me get a look here." He returned to his van and came back with a powerful lantern he used in his carpenter's work. After he'd eased his way down the bank to survey the damage, his head popped up beside the road. "Whooee! You sure done yourself some harm. Your friend's got a cracked ankle and maybe a concussion. I haven't seen nothin' like this since Vee-et-nam."

"Nam?" Hot Dog choked out.

"Oh, yes. Long time ago, but I still remember most of my medic training. Not a good idea to move him ourselves. Got to get an ambulance and a tow truck. You aimin' to stay here, or you want to ride with me? If I was you, I'd stay. Ridin' around on these roads is enough to kill a feller anyway." He looked sharply at Hot Dog who merely nodded and lay back on the soft grass.

It was probably another hour before Harvey returned, riding with the tow truck driver, an EMT van and a Sheriff's car close behind. By that time Hot Dog was so exhausted and in so much pain that even the Sheriff's car looked good to him.

It took the emergency responders quite a while, but they managed to get Conner onto a board with a collar around his neck and slowly lever him back up to the road. After sliding him into the EMT van, they helped Hot Dog climb in beside him. They didn't want to give him painkillers until he'd been thoroughly examined to make sure his cracked ribs hadn't done any internal damage. Ironically, he'd have given anything for some Hydrocodone laced with Demerol.

—⁓—

The ambulance made a relatively quick trip to Chamber's hospital in Danville. While their combined injuries weren't life threatening, they were too serious for immediate release. After Hot Dog's ribs had been taped and Conner's ankle had been set, they were moved to a double room for overnight observation. Conner was muttering incoherently, obviously confused from the concussion. Hot Dog couldn't think of any of Conner's relatives, but he gave the nurse his own mother's number with instructions for a set of clean clothes. Then he finally collapsed into a deep, drugged sleep.

Back at the accident site, the tow truck driver and the Sheriff's Deputy who had taken the call made an executive decision. They would wait until daylight to pull the damaged Rover up the bank. The job would be hard enough then, and there was no reason to spend possible hours trying to retrieve it in the dark. Nope. It would wait. Besides, they needed to get Harvey back to Danville to pick up his own van and go on about his business. The Deputy wrote down the plate number to run it for a stolen vehicle check, and they headed back to Danville.

Harvey rode in the Deputy's car since he had left his van in the Yell County parking lot. They chatted about the accident and repeated all the local gossip each man knew, especially the juicy stuff. "Them fellers is lucky," Harvey expounded. "There's been more deer hit this year than I ever remember. They like to come down to the river for water just about dark. A few more feet and those boys'd have been in the water."

Just before he got out of the car, Harvey had a memory flash. "Say, he said," I just remembered. I saw another set of tracks down there at the wreck when I went down to check on that fellar. I think there was three of those boys."

The Deputy perked up. Harvey had been a scout in Nam, and he was well known in these parts as an excellent tracker. The footprints at the scene were all tramped over by now, so they couldn't verify the tip, but he figured Harvey knew what he was talking about. He hurried inside to check for recent alerts on the computer system and hit the jackpot! A BOLO for three men in a Range Rover, matching license plate and all. The phones began ringing in Danville, Dardanelle and Russellville, and the chase was on!

—〰—

Early the next morning, a still groggy Hot Dog was picking at his breakfast and waiting for the doctor and his mother when Sheriff Wilson of Yell County entered his room. "Are you Royce Haynes?" he demanded. When Hot Dog nodded, he continued,"You are under arrest for delivery of an illegal substance, possession with intent to deliver, fleeing prosecution, and anything else I can add on!"

Janis Haynes was shocked when she arrived with the clothes to find Royce had already been moved to the Danville jail. She raced to the Sheriff's office with alarm bells ringing in her mind. *What was wrong? How had this happened? What went wrong? What had Royce not told her?* She was flummoxed when she couldn't see or talk to him because he 'was still being questioned'. Bill Wilson was an old friend, but he left a message that he'd have to talk to her later. So, she did what any anxious mother would do, and called the best layer she knew. She informed a Deputy that a lawyer was on the way, and any questioning was to stop. She only hoped Royce would keep his mouth shut until he had representation. The Deputy didn't say yes, and he didn't say no, but he did take the clean change of clothes since he was pretty sure Hot Dog would be needing them.

34

When Chet left the scene of the wreck, his mind was rushing in several directions. He figured the chances of hitch hiking out of the area tonight were slim, so he headed back to the trailer to regroup and prepare for what he was sure was coming. The way he figured it, they'd be all over the place come morning. He'd have a only a few hours to get ahead of them, and he'd have to deal with the probability of dogs, even in this rough terrain.

He hurried back down the road toward the narrow turn off. He was almost there when he heard a car coming, and quickly slid into the steep ditch to hide. As soon as the car passed, he jumped up and sprinted for the driveway. He was sure now that Conner and Hot Dog would be getting help. That was one less thing for him to worry about. He was on his own for sure now, and it was up to him to make a plan.

Back at the trailer, he fumbled under the well cover for the spare key and slipped through the front door. He could get a little rest here and leave first thing before day light. If they had dogs, they'd find him in about an hour, so he had to get gone on the fly. He didn't bother with turning on water or electricity; he could run enough water out of the shut off water heater for the night, and he had enough food bars for three days. *Shit! How did things get so screwed up? Murder? No way. There is something really wrong here! I've got to get back to Russellville. Maybe not. Someone up there is killing people, and I'm getting blamed for it. Mexico makes more sense.*

Chet searched the trailer with his lantern looking for anything that might help him escape. He had food bars, but water was too heavy to carry. He'd take one quart bottle; after that he'd have to risk the local streams. No telling what kind of bacteria and toxins were in them. He rummaged in the medicine cabinet and found an old bottle of antibiotics. He poured them into a side pocket of his backpack along with the snake-bite kit and a first-aid kit. A master knife and a small axe were already in the pack where he stored them. Although he didn't expect to use them he took along a butane lighter, some extra kitchen knives and a one-egg frying pan. He rolled up several yards of wire and light rope and stuffed them into the backpack too.

The pack was getting heavy, but he couldn't use the pockets in his cargo pants because he expected to have to wade the river. Finally, he cut the camo tent into two big rectangles, one to sit on and one to cover him, then tied them to the rack of the backpack. Exhausted, he set his watch and climbed onto one of the beds for four hours of sleep.

When he awakened he ate a food bar and drank some water. He waited until he could just see the trees outside, then he locked the door and put the key back before he started down the rocky path to the river.

By the time he got down to the river the sun was just visible over the near mountains. He set his backpack down and walked up river, back, then down the river to confuse the dogs. Then he tied his hiking boots around his neck and started wading upstream. He crawled out on the far side and walked back and forth as he had before. Then he stepped back into the water and crossed to the side he started from making his way up onto the rocky bluffs where he would be hard to track.

Chet continued his pattern of zig-zagging over rocks, returning to the Fourche River, then climbing high for more zig-zagging until late morning. On his last pass, he emptied his aching bladder into the river one last time so his scent would be washed away. Then he filled his now empty water bottle with river water and started back up the bluff. He found a small cavity in the rocks with a nice overhang and crawled in out of the sun. He was exhausted from the heat and humidity and the difficulty of climbing up and down the often treacherous bluffs staying alert for poisonous snakes. Long past his adrenalin high, he spread his camo cloth and backed up against the cool rock wall where he swallowed an antibiotic pill and soon fell into a fitful sleep.

35

Unfortunately, the hunt for Chet was slow getting started. First, the tow truck broke a cable pulling the Rover back up onto the road. Then a CSI team went over it carefully trying to find evidence of a third person. There was one pair of men's dress shoes piled into the back of the Rover. Perhaps they belonged to the third man. Then, they had to figure which way the man went. Even if Royce and Conner were talking to the police, which they weren't, they had been down under the bank and couldn't really know. So, they decided to bring in the dogs from Little Rock. That took over two hours. Meanwhile Harvey was enlisted to try to pick up the trail. Logically, Chet would have crossed the bridge to avoid having to cross the river again later. But Harvey couldn't find any sign of him on that side. Only an idiot would have jumped into the river in the dark, so the third man must have backtracked.

When the dogs finally arrived, they were given the shoes to sniff, and sure enough they started back down the road in the direction the three men had come from. They sniffed an area of the ditch several times, and Harvey guessed the man had hidden there briefly. Soon the dogs went off the road into a narrow rutty trail that led straight upward. By the time they reached the trailer at the top, the whole group of Sheriff's officers were totally winded.

They followed the dogs down the steep, rocky hill on the other side until they reached the river. There the dogs began to behave peculiarly. First they ran up the river bank, then back the other way. Finally they sat down on the bank panting and whining. The river was shallow there, so the handlers took the dogs across, but they didn't pick up Chet's scent on the other side.

Considering the steepness of the banks and the large sheets of rock, the dogs were unlikely to be of further use now. The frustrated men knew their quarry was likely still in the immediate vicinity, probably holed up along the river somewhere. This was going to require a massive man hunt unless they could smoke him out some other way. While they were discussing alternatives, it began to rain.

By the time the discouraged hunters climbed all the way back up to the trailer and down to their cars, the rain had set in pretty good. They all knew that if it continued, the scent would be mostly washed away, and the dogs would be useless. Bill Wilson sent the dogs and their handlers back to Little Rock, and he and Curly McCurly began to work on plan B.

—◊◊◊—

Plan B was to bring in a State Police or Little Rock Police helicopter. There was enough space between the mountains and high bluffs here to fly a helicopter safely. A pilot and a trained observer could cover a lot of ground in an hour or two. Curly agreed to make the calls.

He struck out with the State Police. They had two helicopters on standby, but only one pilot who was required to be available for State emergencies. The other crews were at Fort Bragg in Texas for a week of intensive training. The situation at the Little Rock Police was almost as bad. One of their helicopters was on standby, but they didn't have a qualified pilot. That's when Sheriff McCurly remembered Clay Bridgewater.

Clay was off-again, on-again "companion" of Hattie West, the forensic expert. He was a retired Air Force test pilot who had tested Wineparkers among other things. He had once remarked that his most prized possession was an autographed picture of Chuck Yager. If they could get him, he was one hell of a pilot!

The Sheriff had Hattie West's number in his phone, but there wasn't any service. Then when he got close enough to Danville, he got her voice mail. He left an urgent message about their predicament then headed back to Danville to wait. He'd done a lot of waiting in his career, but it never got easier.

—ⵑ—

When the two Sheriffs arrived back at Danville they were accosted by an almost hysterical Janis Haynes. She had been waiting all day for a chance to talk to Sheriff Wilson who had quite unexpectedly refused to see her earlier in the day. She hadn't seen Royce, and she hadn't been able to pry any information from the local staff. Not only that, but the lawyer she had called was in court and couldn't come until tomorrow morning. She was fit to be tied!

Sheriff Wilson listened to her verbal assault with practiced patience then explained that Royce was being held as a material witness. "How can that be?" Janis confronted him pointedly. "How could he be a material witness, for Chrissakes when all he did was go on a fishing trip?"

"Well," the Sheriff explained, "We think he may have been the last one to see a murder suspect."

"Murder? What murder? Not my boy. Not Royce!"

"Now, now, Janis," Sheriff Wilson soothed. "We don't think Royce is a murderer. But we do think he may know enough to help us apprehend a fugitive."

"Did he tell you that? You can't question him without a lawyer! I've called George Denton from Little Rock, and he won't be able to come until tomorrow morning."

"Not to worry, Janis. We'll make him nice and comfortable for tonight, and I promise we won't question him until George Denton gets here tomorrow."

"Don't you JANIS me!" She retorted. "I'll see you tomorrow morning, and you've got some explaining to do, BILL!" She turned on her heels and stomped out to her big red Cadillac where she slammed the door and headed back to Dardanelle.

Sheriff McCurly called in to Russellville and was relieved that things were pretty much in line up there. He told Sheriff Wilson he'd be in touch just as soon as he had more information about a helicopter for tomorrow morning. Then he climbed into his car and headed back to Russellville.

36

Janis Haynes was in a royal snit as she sped from Danville back to Dardanelle. That son-of-a-bitch Bill Wilson would never be elected again if she had anything to do with it! But right now she had a bigger problem on her hands. She wanted Royce out of that jail NOW! She had anticipated that he might be arrested because he was with Chet, but not that he would be held as a material witness. She was sure he knew enough not to say anything until she sent him a lawyer. But this could go on for some time. No one knew where in the hell that bastard, Chet, was. And she'd have to be ready to keep him from talking when they found him. Connor was probably safe. He didn't know enough to be much of a threat, and he also knew to keep his mouth shut.

When she turned into her driveway out at the lake, her lights bounced over Royce's Lexus and the big red Vette. She ground her teeth thinking about Chet. She wasn't through with him yet. He might go down for murder, but he wasn't taking her Royce with him!

She unlocked her door and headed straight for the medicine cabinet where she swallowed a Nexium and a Prozac. That should keep her for a while. She had Ambien if she needed it later. Right now she had work to do. First, she made several calls on a burner phone using her voice distorter. Then she began to go through the house collecting anything even marginally incriminating for quick destruction. She carried her bag of papers and books along with the phone to the Vette. Then she pulled on a pair of gloves before she unlocked Royce's apartment and went to a prearranged hidey hole where she emptied the contents into another bag.

After she had pulled on a hoodie, she drove slowly out to Delaware Bay to the public boat ramp. She considered it an omen that a fire was already lit in the trash barrel by the ramp. She didn't see anyone around, but she hurried to dispose of her contraband. She stayed just long enough to be sure that the fire had done its work, then she drove to the old Lilac cemetery and walked to Eddie's grave. She looked around furtively then opened a small cache at the base of his headstone. She quickly inserted some accounting records and her "little black book". Then she headed back home to plan her schedule for showing real estate tomorrow.

Janis routinely called on Royce to back her up at the office, but she needed tomorrow off to go back to Danville to get Royce released. She finally patched a schedule together with two other realtors and began to relax a little. *Not to panic. Not to panic.* She repeated her mantra in her head, but the fact of the matter was that she was genuinely panicked, and she spent most of her night sitting in her big recliner stewing over a situation that was rapidly spiraling out of control. Her husband was in his grave; Royce was in jail; and she was entirely alone.

When Eddie had been alive they had owned a small realty firm and had made a decent living. When MNSU was built on some of their property, they made a killing. Looking to the future, they invested wisely in rental property and the Lizard Stop convenience store. They were planning to build their own apartment complex too. But Eddie keeled over with a heart attack and died, so everything had come to a screeching halt.

About a year after Eddie's death, she was at a realty convention sharing some righteous weed with an old friend. He casually asked her what she was planning to do with the insurance settlement that was rumored to be $100,000 or more. Then he casually suggested a way to double that nest egg. He described an "organization" currently doing business in Arkansas that wanted to expand. They carried two products: Hydrocodone and high grade "medical" marijuana. The deal was simple. She would place orders using a burner phone with a voice modulator. The goods would be delivered to blind drop boxes. All she had to do was package and retail. Of course she'd need to pay in advance, but that was already arranged too. She paid against a fake invoice from a convenience market supply company in the Rio Grande Valley. It appeared to be totally legitimate. And, the Lizard Stop was a perfect cover. No checks; only cash and credit cards. As long as she kept a legitimate set of books for tax purposes, she could deposit cash regularly without anyone's being the wiser. As the drugs were delivered to the blind drops, Royce, in his Hot Dog disguise, picked them up. It was a very efficient operation.

After about a year of undetected dealing, her realty friend suggested she could more than double her profits if she set up a designer lab. The products would be very desirable to the local market. And she could sell anonymously to other dealers using the Rio Grande network. Pow! The business was off and running. She paid Chet, Conner, and Edith in cash. No records there. Royce took his share in real estate mostly, plus a few expensive toys like his Lexus and his boat. Then Royce had almost killed that Stapleton kid in the hospital, and Edith had tried to rip off the business, and that dammed deer had run in front of the Rover, and...

When she reached the Yell County Center in Dardanelle, she sat in her car waiting for the lawyer and trying to calm down. She had one goal today, and that was to get Royce out of jail!

When the attorney from Little Rock arrived, she climbed out of her Cadillac, ripping her hose in the process, and scrambled across the lot. Thankfully, the attorney was very calm. This should be a routine procedure. All she had to do was take a few deep breaths and wait outside while he cleared things up. If she'd just be patient she would be talking to Royce within the hour. She declined his suggestion to go get some coffee while she waited and pretended to be reading the book she had brought just in case.

As the time wore on Janis sensed a change of mood in the reception area. She had known these people for many years, but she felt them withdrawing. Their demeanor was definitely cooler than when she first arrived. What she couldn't know was that back in his office Sheriff Wilson had received a game-changing call from Sheriff McCurly. The CSI report from the torched lab had just come in. Fingerprints from Chet, Connor and Royce had been found on the toilet seat. The rest of the lab was clean. The most plausible explanation was that the guys had taken off their gloves when they urinated. After all, it's dammed hard to unzip your pants with gloves on.

When the high priced attorney emerged form the back, he was clearly less confident than when he entered. He led her outside to give her the news. Royce was being charged as an accessory to murder. Bail had not been set. Janis would not have a conversation with Royce today.

37

Clay Bridgewater and Hattie West had just finished making love when Sheriff McCurly called. It wasn't the same as it had been 20 years ago when they first met, but it was still good. She was younger than he was and still had a healthy libido. He hated to admit that his had declined over the years so that sex was no longer his number one priority, but it was still up there, so to speak.

Hattie was grilling some fresh fish a friend had brought her, and Clay was cutting up a garden salad with big chunks of avocado. She turned the fish and picked up her phone to check her messages. She recognized Sheriff McCurly's number and punched 'return call'. After he explained what he needed, she passed the phone to Clay. "Your services are requested," she smiled knowingly.

"Hey, Clay," Curly started. "What are you up to these days?"

"What can I do for you?" Clay returned. "From the way Hattie is looking at me, you must have a mission in mind."

Curly explained their current dilemma and asked Clay if he or anyone else he knew could fly for them tomorrow morning. Clay said he'd need to line up a good copilot and promised to call back.

Clay called his old buddy, Jeremy Boyd, who had flown search and rescue with him last year when flash floods had trapped home owners near Lake Ouichita. They agreed to meet in Little Rock early in the morning and fly over to meet Sheriff McCurly at the Forche Mountain Camp Ground near where Chet had been seen last.

—⟪⟫—

Chet was awakened from his long nap by cold water dripping onto his face. It had started to rain while he was asleep and enough water had accumulated up top to begin dripping through the layers of rocks. Chet didn't mind the rain at all. Let it drip on him all it wanted. It would very soon wash away his scent if it continued. Then he'd have a chance to make it to the campground without having to cross the Forche again.

The good fortune of rain cheered him considerably. He still ached from all the physical exertion of the day. He had lost track of how many times he had tracked back and forth along the river's bank then up a slippery bluff. He ate three food bars to celebrate and drank some water he'd dipped out of the river. Then he set his watch for 5:00 am and fell into a much needed, quiet sleep.

The rain stopped during the night. When he awakened, he sat quietly, meditating to calm himself. Then, with just enough light coming over the mountains, he climbed up onto the top of the ridge and hurriedly moved along beside the river. He figured he was less than halfway to the campground and transportation. If he could make it to the next bridge over the Forche, he could wait until night to follow the road into the campground, hoping no one would see him or be suspicious.

—⁓—

Clay was relieved that the rain had stopped. He would be very reluctant to fly in the rain, especially in the mountains where pockets of ground fog could throw you off course. As soon as the light was good he and Jeremy took off for the Ouichitas. He planned to meet Sheriff McCurly and Sheriff Wilson at the big pasture just past the campground between 8:30 and 9:00.

Both Sheriffs were there. McCurly had gathered several pictures of Chet together with his physical description. "We figure," he explained, "that he's heading for this campground. I don't know if he can make it today or not. It's mighty rough up there. But he's probably following the bluffs along the river. If he hears something he'll have some chance to hide in the trees. Fly over everything several times. If nothing else, it'll slow him down so we can get set up along the road leading in. There's a narrow place between the bluff and that little creek that feeds into the Forche. We'll try to trap him there."

Clay and Jeremy worked the bluffs between the two bridges. They caught a flash of movement on their second pass toward the camp ground, but Chet's camouflage squares from the tent saved him. The helicopter flew on by. He moved quickly then, trying to cover some ground before it came back. He had no doubt they were looking for him. Several times he made a fast dive for cover as the helicopter suddenly crested a ridge.

Clay and Jeremy landed again on the big field. "He's out there all right. We caught a glimpse of him twice, but he's well camouflaged. You were right. He's headed for the bridge. But he'll have to wait until dark to cross. Besides, that little creek is starting to bubble up from all the rain we've been having. He may have trouble crossing it."

The helicopter had just lifted off again when Clay got a message from State Police Headquarters. "We've, got some flash flooding in your area, and we sure could use a pair of eyes in the sky. Are you game?"

"Sure. Be happy to help, but I'm getting low on fuel."

"There's a little air strip just west of Danville out toward Magazine. They can fix you up there, I'm pretty sure. I'll give you the GPS coordinates."

Clay and Jeremy looked at each other and simultaneously hunched their shoulders in a "What's a man to do gesture?" Then they headed north-east toward Danville.

—〰—

Chet was relieved when the helicopter quit working the area. He had spent too much time hiding today. Still he should reach the highway before dark. His intuition told him that there'd be police at the camp and probably all along the road. They'd be expecting him to wait until dark to make his move. He had to find some way to get around them.

As he neared the bridge, he was cut off by a creek that was bubbling high from last night's rain. When he saw a small log floating by, he made his plan. Wading out as far as he dared, he waited for a discouragingly long time. Then he saw it, a larger log moving in line with the current. He waited until it was about 30 yards upstream then made his move. Leaving his back pack behind, he jumped into the water and back-stroked until the log approached him. Then he grabbed a protruding branch. To his dismay, it pulled off leaving him sputtering with surprise. He recovered quickly and grabbed the end of the log as it went by. Working very slowly, he half swam and half crawled his way to the middle being very careful to stay on the side away from the bluffs where he assumed the man hunt was taking place.

Chet was almost to the river where he hoped to float under the bridge completely unnoticed. He ducked his head as low as possible without

drowning and held on tight. He had no way of pre-
dicting which way the log would swing when it met
the river, so he planned to hang on for dear life and
ride it through. That was when he heard the unbe-
lievably loud rushing of water. **FLASH FLOOD**!

The raging waters lifted his log and flung it back
and forth as he entered the river where more logs
and debris were caroming off the banks and split-
ting up on big boulders in the water. He passed several camp sites where screaming parents were trying to gather children and run for higher ground.
He held on as long as he could. Then he let go!

Chet had no idea where the river was taking him. He struggled toward the tree-lined bank
where he might be able to grab onto a tree branch,
but the waves were washing over his head and he
was barely able to breathe. He saw the big catalpa on
the bank just in time to duck. He felt an enormous
blow to his abdomen and struggled in the water
before he realized he had been swept onto a large
underwater branch that was blocking his movement down stream. Frantically he clawed at the
branch, barely able to hang on and resist the pounding water behind him. Eventually he managed to
move up to the main trunk where he grabbed on to
a sturdy branch above him. He clung to the branch
while the force of the water kept sweeping his feet
off the underwater branch he was using as a brace.
He knew he didn't have much strength left so he
made a final effort to lift himself out of the water
onto a higher branch which he was able to straddle

and hang on to. He was too tired and too scared to try to move again so he stayed there clinging to his branch during a miserable night.

—∿∿—

The law officers assembled for the man hunt immediately abandoned their positions when the flooding started. They raced back to the camp grounds to help the struggling families to safety. It was growing dark and the search for Chet was completely abandoned. He might be walking across the bridge right now for all they knew, but he was no longer top priority. Sheriff Wilson set up a command center and organized his men and local Forest Rangers who where hurrying into the area. Although it had been a narrow escape, every one was eventually accounted for, even the dogs. The distraught families began loading up their camping equipment and heading out. A few had lost items that had been close to the river when the flood hit, but very few wished to stay to hunt for them in the morning.

Clay and Jeremy flew the helicopter back to the small air field where Sheriff McCurly picked them up in his car and took them with him back to Russellville. He'd bring them back early tomorrow morning when their sky eyes would play an important part in search and rescue in the area as needed.

—∿∿—

The capture of Chet was rather anticlimactic. Clay and Jeremy spotted him in his tree and flew over several times to verify his identity. He had lost his rifle some time ago and was no longer considered armed and dangerous. But the water was still too rough to bring a motor boat in to get him, so Clay dropped Chet a line and yelled to him to climb into the attached leg harness. Chet was too tired and clumsy by now to put up any fight. It was all he could muster to buckle one leg at a time into the harness. In fact, the soggy bedraggled prisoner didn't look anything at all like a high flying drug designer.

38

Sheriff McCurly, Garnet, and Hattie White sat around his conference table trying to gather loose ends. "This is a mess," McCurly complained. "There are several scenarios, and none of them holds up all the way."

"Let's start the way we usually do, with what we know," Hattie prompted pulling the easel board closer to the table. "We start with the river party. Edith and/or Jim Stafford had ordered drugs, which were delivered by Chet." She wrote their names on the board with arrows from Chet toward Edith and Jim. "Then Dan Stapleton stole the drugs, got snakebit, and lost them."

"Then Colleen and I found the drugs which had been laced with Demerol," Garnet continued. "Our designer drugs. Following that, Royce, AKA Hot Dog, sells Colleen a Phenergan-laced joint that almost kills Dan. Our designers again." Dan's, Hot Dog's and Colleen's names were added to the board. Dan and Colleen were placed to the side on an arc to indicate indirect involvement.

"We know now that Conner Drummond was helping Chet with the design work based on fingerprints at the drug lab and other circumstantial evidence. We also found Hot Dog's fingerprints at the lab, and we have the photo ID's from Colleen and her shots of the Rover, and Valentine's pics with the Rover at the house," McCurly summed up.

"But what we don't know is where the drugs came from. We've documented that both Chet and Conner cheated on prescriptions to get Phenergan now and then. We think we've traced the Demerol back to a supplier in Morocco via Canada. But where did the Hydrocodone come from? We thought we had it licked when our CI, Jim Stafford tipped us to the two mules out of Searcy." Here he was interrupted as the women chimed in, "JIM? You've got to be kidding!"

"No we turned him after Hattie analyzed that bottle with his name on it. He was the one who set up Edith after Dan called him to meet at Mulberry Hall to get the drugs back. Maybe he thought we'd arrest her and get her off his back about getting more drugs with his name on them. Any way," he paused to catch his breath, "We didn't get diddly-squat out of those two mules. They told their stories then clammed up. We had them for possession with intent to deliver and set their bail really high. But damned if some fancy lawyer didn't show up with the money. That's when we knew someone with big bucks wanted to keep them happy and quiet."

"Did you get anything from Searcy?" Garnet asked.

"Yes and no. The task force had their eye on a fellow named Brady who was running a small shoe store up there, but when they showed up he was already gone. Someone tipped him in a hurry. But we found a bunch of Muniquita shoes. We didn't know what that was about until Alyssia Bergamont opened that shipment at her shop. Somebody was shipping Hydrocodone into the area inside shoe boxes."

"Any idea who?" Garnet was eager for more information.

"Yes and no, again. We tried tracing Alyssia's shoes back through the delivery system; they became real cooperative when they knew there was possible prison time involved. But we came up empty handed. We worked all the way back to Harlengen, Texas, down near the border. All the DEA found was an empty shoe store. One of the shop keepers in the area said the owner had to leave suddenly because his mother was dying in Mexico! Can you believe it?"

"But you said yes too," Hattie prodded.

"Ah," he pointed his finger as if to refresh his memory. "We found fingerprints belonging to Jim and Edith on Alyssia's back door sill."

"So if Jim and Edith were bringing in drugs for Chet and Conner to alter, and they're paying our boys big bucks, then why would Chet murder them?" Hattie questioned.

"That's where it falls apart," McCurly admitted. "Unless there was some kind of turf war going on, I just can't see killing the golden goose, uh gooses, uh geese," he stammered. "Besides, after we picked up those two out of Searcy, nothing changed. We had just as much, if not more designer stuff on the streets."

"What if the Searcy shipment was for Jim and Edith, and Chet and Conner had to get something else in fast when it was picked up?" Hattie asked.

"We think that's probably what happened. That shipment of shoes to Alyssia was probably supposed to come in late. Then Jim and Edith would slip in and take the drying packets. But the packets and shoes were already gone; nothing left but an empty packing box!"

"We're not getting where we want to go," Garnet interjected. "Jim and Edith should have been mad enough to hurt somebody. So why did Chet go out there and kill them?"

"I'm having a little trouble with that myself," the Sheriff admitted. "What if Jim's playing both sides against the middle?"

"The Searcy bust explains where some of the Hydrocodone came from, but we're not sure who it was intended for, and why didn't it dent the local supply?" Garnet was puzzled.

"We found fingerprints of Brady Collins, AKA Don Harrington, AKA ...; you know the drill. He's been in the system for several years in Texas and Oklahoma. This is the first time we've picked him up in Arkansas. He's known to travel with a woman partner. We figure she was dealing too, but out of a different location. Right now we can't locate either of them."

"That would seem to rule out Edith and Jim as the main suppliers, since they would have lost both the Searcy and the Dardanelle connection," Garnet reasoned.

"OK," Hattie continued. "We don't think Chet and Conner had a good reason to kill Jim and Edith and trash their own place. What about Hot Dog?"

"Hot Dog is a bit of a problem," the Sheriff admitted. "We can't use the ID from Colleen's photo in a court of law because she saw him in disguise and didn't recognize him when she saw him again, and other than his being with Chet and Conner, we don't really have much on him. No fingerprints, except the lab, no sightings, just mostly circumstantial evidence. We're hoping Dan Stapelton will come forward to ID him, but Dan may not have seen him when he wasn't in disguise. We'll never make accessory to murder stick unless we can place him at the scene, especially since we're not even sure Chet is the actual murderer. His lawyer knows it, and it looks like we're going to have to release him on bail."

'I don't get it," Hattie was puzzled. "Aren't we sure Chet's Vette was at both scenes?"

"Yeah, but we don't know for sure Chet was in it. That car was wiped down. Why would he wipe his own car down?"

"Maybe they were all three in it," Garnet offered.

"We've been looking into that. Based on Jim's wife's finding him and Edith about 7:30, he/they would have had time to get back and leave Dardanelle about 8:30, which is what Janis Haynes told us. But, what little they did tell us, they all said they left in the Rover at 6:30. So ...," he trailed off.

"You think she was protecting her son?"

"That's entirely possible. She said she 'thought' they went to Bull Shoals. That could have been a stall for time."

This was all getting too confusing for Garnet. She tried to get them back on track. "What about a murder weapon?"

"Never found one, and boy did we look! We spent three days searching every nook and cranny within 20 yards of either side of the road. If he threw it out, he sure made a lucky toss."

"What about that unexpected turn around?" Garnet asked.

"No," he shook his head. "Not a thing there either."

"So where does that leave us?" Hattie asked.

"Well, we need to find the gun, and we need to find out who used it. We're releasing Hot Dog (or should I say Royce?) tomorrow morning. Of course we'll keep an eye on him. Meanwhile we got warrants for GPS trackers on both the Lexus and the Vette. Maybe we'll get lucky."

Garnet was still focusing on the turn around. It had to be important, but why? "Is it all right if

Collen and I take another look at the turn around?"
she asked.

"Sure. Knock yourselves out. You found the
drug bottle before. Why not go out and find the
gun, or whatever is hidden out there?" He smiled
in exasperation.

39

Garnet was up early the next morning waiting for Colleen to come in from work. She handed her niece a bagel and a travel cup of coffee, and they headed north toward the murder site and the abandoned house place. They called Olivia Hubbard along the way, but got only static and bells on the line. Olivia was surprised and pleased to see them. Leaving her pail of dog chow for the emus at the barn door, she crossed the lot and invited them in for coffee.

"How 'bout an hour from now?" Garnet suggested. "We want to go on up to the old house place to have a look around. We probably won't find anything, but we're anxious to try."

"That's perfect," Olivia smiled. "I still have to go up to the north pens; and that'll give me plenty of time to make a fresh pot of coffee when I get back."

The road was muddy as usual, and Garnet and Colleen could see the tracks where a tractor had straddled some of the ruts, but there were no new tracks in the lane to the old barn.

"OK," Garnet instructed as she climbed down from the truck, "Let's take a fresh look at this.

Where would I be if I were something the murderer hid? If the murderer retrieved something, we're obviously not going to find it."

They began by looking in the obvious places the Sheriff's team had already searched: the old rock chimney where the house had been, inside old tin cans, etc. The only thing they found in the dilapidated barn were a rusty manure fork and some crumbling bird's nests plus a few piles of what appeared to be human feces and shredded tissues left by hikers who made emergency stops.

About the time Garnet and Colleen started looking outside the building, Olivia was just coming back to the barn. She heard a car on the gravel road and looked out just in time to see a red flash head in the same direction as Garnet and Colleen. She dashed toward the house and breathlessly called 911 only to hear buzzing and bells on her line. *Damned phone is out again.* What could she do? She quickly grabbed the keys to the flatbed and ran back to the barn to start it.

Garnet and Colleen had given up for all practical purposes. Colleen decided to go back into the barn to take advantage of the "facilities", and Garnet kicked around outside waiting for her. As she leaned against the front of her truck, she glanced casually at the old well pipe nearby. She had looked down into it earlier, of course, but had seen nothing. This time she looked again. There was something reflecting along the stem of the honeysuckle vine that grew beside it. Garnet was intrigued and moved closer to see what it could be. There was a brown/black string wrapped around the vine and covered by its leaves. As she lifted the string and followed it down across the lip of the well pipe, she felt a weight on it. She held her breath as she slowly reeled the line up. And there it was, a black net bag that had been invisible from the top. Inside it were a Colt 45 and a pair of vinyl gloves!

Garnet had just hooked the bag over the ring finger of her left hand when she heard a woman's voice saying, "I'll take that. You don't have any use for it."

Garnet whirled to see Janis Haynes crossing the yard with a Smith and Wesson 38 held firmly in her hand. She had been so intent on the well pipe that she hadn't heard Janis approaching. Janis had seen Garnet's tire tracks in the lane and had left the Vette just out of site while she came in on foot catching Garnet completely by surprise. *Holy shit!!*

"You!" Garnet gasped. "You killed them and started the fire. Why?"

"I had my reasons. Several hundred thousand, if you must know. And that stupid Edith thought she could horn in on me."

"And Jim?"

"That snake was nothing but a 'confidential informant'," she spat out the words.

"But why start the fire?" Garnet tried to keep Janis talking, playing for time while she searched her shocked brain for something to try. She slowly backed away from the well, pulling Janis with her so that her back was turned away from the barn. With any luck, Colleen would stay out of sight and not get hurt by this stone killer, but live to deliver justice.

"That's easy, Dr. Genius," Janis mocked her. "To set up that stupid Chet. Oh, he thought he was so special with his big house and his fancy car, looking down his nose at the stupid little real estate agent who set him up. But this stupid little real estate agent knew enough to keep some extra keys. It was his gun from his house, and his car that came up here for the kill, and it's his car that came up here today. And, it's his gun in that bag. Now give it to me!"

"Why do you need it now?" Garnet asked in a puzzled tone.

"Lady, you are some dolt for a college professor. I need it to shoot you."

Garnet couldn't help gasping out loud.

"I have good information that Mr. Chet will be bailed out this afternoon. Not too long after that the Sheriff will get an anonymous call about a certain gun that just happens to be in a certain red Vette that just happens to have the right kind of mud on the tires. And, as even you can see, the bullets from Edith and Jim, and now from you too, whenever they find you, will just happen to be from that gun. Now give it here. And don't even think about trying any funny stuff. I have a permit for this gun (She waved the Smith and Wesson toward Garnet.), and I know how to use it."

Garnet faced her killer and slowly sank to her knees, cradling the gun against her chest over her heart.

"Get up you bitch!" Janis commanded.

"I can't. I'm too scared," Garnet stuttered, not knowing if Janis would come within grabbing range. For all her threats, Janis couldn't afford to shoot Garnet with her Smith and Wesson. A concealed weapon permit meant the gun was registered to her.

Unseen by either Garnet or Janis, Colleen knelt breathlessly behind the barn doors. She could just see Janis through a crack in the door. She made a rough calculation of the distance and tightened her grip on the old manure fork in anticipation. The handle was old and rotten and crumbling in her hands. Then she moved quietly toward Janis' back pointing the fork straight at her.

The startled Janis swung around full face toward the rapidly advancing Colleen and hesitated slightly before she swung the barrel of the gun away from Garnet and toward her.

As if on cue, Colleen screamed like a banshee and lifted the tines of the fork and thrust them directly toward Janis' chest. As Janis' arms went up in a protective reflex, Colleen twisted the manure fork and swung it sideways, baseball fashion, across her middle. Janis dropped the gun as the fork slammed across her abdomen then rolled onto the ground with both Colleen and Garnet trying to grab her ankles.

Janis kicked Garnet hard in the chin and rolled free. She managed to pick up the gun then turned and ran, firing two random shots behind her. She made a beeline back down the lane and jumped into the Vette. With great roaring and slinging of gravel, she managed to turn the Vet around and headed back toward the highway knocking the low bottom of the car on roots and ruts along the way.

Garnet and Colleen raced to the pickup and sped back down the road in hot pursuit. The pickup was better adapted to the ruts and ridges, but it nearly shook the women's teeth out as they hit every ridge trying to catch up to the faster Vette. Garnet was in tears from the pain and jostling of her kicked jaw.

They had just rounded the last muddy curve before the Y in the road, when Garnet slammed on the brakes, skidding and fish-tailing to a stop turned back the wrong way. The pain slowed Garnet down, but Colleen jumped out of the truck and charged down the road.

Olivia had parked her big flatbed across the road cutting off any escape. Janis had made a desperate try to squeeze through the trees past the truck only to high center the Vette on an old stump and knock herself out in the process.

Colleen opened the driver's door and yanked Janis out dragging her to the ground on her stomach. "Quick," she yelled at Olivia. "Get something to tie her up with. We can't let her get away. She has a gun!"

The three women had just finished hog tying Janis with a roll of bailing twine when the Sheriff's car came barreling down the road with sirens on and lights flashing. Sheriff McCurly could hardly believe his eyes. He looked at Janis all trussed up with bailing twine, Colleen with her foot in the middle of Janis' back, Garnet with a huge blue bruise on her jaw holding a Smith and Wesson, and Olivia swinging her legs as she sat on the edge of the flatbed as if nothing in the world were wrong.

"We were just going to call you," Olivia joked. "But the phone is out, and we hadn't made it down to the bridge yet." Then she turned serious, "How did you know we were here?"

"We put a GPS tracker on the Vette yesterday because we knew we'd probably be releasing Chet on bail today. That was quite a surprise when ole Chet was still in jail this morning, but his Vette was moving. The tracker went dead at the same place that Edith's did when we were tracking her. So we figured we'd better get up here."

—∞—

After Sheriff McCurly had arrested Janis and headed back toward Russellville, the three women began to settle down, except for Garnet's frequent trips to the bathroom. They were simultaneously exhausted from the ordeal and jubilant that they had played a part in the capture. A prime topic in their relieved chatter was how close both Garnet and Colleen had come to being shot.

"How did you know to go for her chest?" Garnet asked Colleen.

"Easy." Colleen responded matter-of-factly, "I learned that from wrestling with Tommy Decker. He used to fake me out every time. You see, most girls learn early to protect their boobs. So if you go for the chest, they'll throw their arms up automatically. Then you duck down low, and you've got 'em!"

40

Colleen helped her Aunt Garnet into the passenger's side of the truck and took over the driving. She decided to take her directly to the emergency room since the kicked jaw seemed to be getting bigger and more bruised looking by the minute. Garnet muttered something about going straight home which Colleen ignored.

About half way back to town Garnet stopped dozing long enough to talk. "Colleen, I still can't get over how scared I was. I thought she was really going to shoot me."

"Scared?" Colleen asked incredulously. "You were cool as ice, especially when you kept rotating around that pipe so I could attack her from the back."

"I wasn't trying to line her up for you. I was trying to keep her from seeing you. I don't know how I'd make it if she'd shot you. You were the brave one, screaming like a banshee and running after her with that broken manure fork!"

Colleen reached slowly across the seat and gently took her aunt's hand. "I guess we make a pretty good team, don't we?"

—∿∿—

The wait at the emergency room was much too long. Garnet had run out of adrenalin and began succumbing to pain before she was seen by a doctor. The doctor had her bite down on a tongue depressor and hold it while he pulled on it forcefully. Then he sent her to X-ray. Finally he sent her home with a prescription for Hydrocodone.

As the two women were leaving the emergency room, Sheriff McCurly approached them. He was genuinely relieved that the jaw wasn't broken, but he winced with sympathetic pain when he saw the size and color of the knot. "I just wanted to make sure you two were OK," he offered. "You sure took a chance out there with Janis Haynes. I would have had to blame myself it something happened to either one of you," he stated gently, crossing his arms across his chest as if to ward off an unknown evil.

"Thank you so much for your concern," Colleen held out her hand in friendship. "I guess we've given you a pretty hard time this summer, but we're a pretty tough pair."

He grinned in acknowledgement.

"Oh, there's one more thing," Colleen added. "Now that we know Janis was involved someway. I should probably pass on some third-hand information. Logan said one of his buddies said that when Janis closed the registers at the Lizard Stop, sometimes she'd add extra cash to the receipts. Now that I've thought about it, I'm wondering if she was laundering money."

41

The summer was almost over. Mica was on his way home, and Colleen was making plans to head back for her senior year at UofA. A few more weeks and Garnet would start back for Med student orientation. Garnet and Colleen were sharing a morning cup of coffee before driving out to the Staley farm to meet Dr. Stephanie Gleason who was bringing the big black snake for release to his home territory.

"Are you sure that's what you want to do?" Garnet asked gently.

"Yes. Logan and I have talked it over, and we're both sure we're going to stay together. So it just makes sense for us to move in together. We're going up this afternoon to find an apartment, since neither of us has a place suitable for both of us," Colleen explained.

"Your mother OK with this?" Garnet queried.

"Yeah," Colleen began, then hedged. "She's not real happy with it, but she says it's my decision. I guess it's a case of do as I say, not do as I do."

Garnet laughed, "Oh, yes. She did have her 'romantic interludes' when she was younger. And just between you and me, I'm not sure she's finished yet. She's got a new man in tow every time I see her."

"I think she uses men for sex," Colleen suggested. "At least she doesn't have to get married the way some women do. She's a romantic, but not a hopeless romantic. Speaking of romance, when's Uncle Mica coming in?"

"Two more days," Garnet smiled. I surely could have used him here this summer."

"Me too! I'm still not sure what was going on part of the time. Did they ever figure out who The Big One is?"

"Well, they're reasonably sure it's Janis Haynes. The forensic accountants from the State are trying to follow the money trail. Your tip about the Lizard Stop gave them a good place to start. The three men had big accounts in Acapulco, but they haven't found most of her money yet. She's claiming she heard Chet say where the gun was, and she went up there to get it before he shot someone else. And when she saw me with the gun, she was afraid I was going to shoot her! I still can't get my mind around it all. I know greed is a big motivator, but murder?"

"Yeah, I thought I'd really screwed the pooch over that marijuana for Dan, but these guys make me look really good."

Garnet frowned, "Not really good, just really lucky."

Colleen shrugged her shoulders in semi-agreement.

They continued the conversation as they climbed into the Dakota. "I guess I'll have to come back to testify," Colleen complained. "I hope it doesn't mess up my semester."

"Me too, Garnet agreed. "It may take them a year to get any of this to trial. But you can be sure that whenever it is, it'll be at the most inconvenient time possible."

"Kind of like surgery?" Colleen grinned.

"You didn't have to remind me of that. I hope this year goes better. It's a long way to the Ladies Room from the Gross Lab."

—·——

They bounced up the gravel drive to the Staley's farm where Dr. Gleason was chatting with Mrs. Staley. "I'd sure like to see that big snake let go," Mrs. Staley told them. "But I've got a ladies Bible study I'd better get too. See you all later."

Stephanie Gleason waited until Mrs. Staley was gone then opened the back of her van. Garnet helped her lift the wire crate out, and together they carried it out to the barn. Stephanie opened the top, and they rolled the crate onto its side to free the big snake. He hesitated at first then slowly uncoiled and slithered toward the barn, flicking his tongue to pick up familiar scents. It didn't take him long to disappear under the weathered barn boards.

"I feel as if we're saying good bye to a friend," Garnet admitted. "This all started with a snake bite, but if it hadn't been for this guy, we'd never have figured out this whole drug thing."

"Yes." Dr. Gleason added, making a play on the snake's scientific name, *Elaphe guttata*. "Just remember, "He *Elaphes* best who *Elaphes* last."

"I can't believe she said that," Colleen complained, rolling her eyes.

"I can't believe she did, either," Garnet agreed. And the two of them walked back to the truck with their arms around each other's shoulders.

The End

AN EXCERPT FROM

BERYL WEALAND'S

NEW BOOK,

DIAMONDBACK

1

It was chilly in the earth house, and Ruby pulled her sweater tighter and crossed her arms across her bony chest. She hated it when it rained because it was almost as gloomy outside as it was deep inside the house.

"It's your fault we have to be down here," she whined to the man slumped on the metal folding chair across the table from her. "You had to go gettin' uppity again. I'd a thought you'd had enough last time. You're lucky he didn't turn them loose straight out like he done then. Sure thing, I thought you was a goin' ta die!"

The light in the narrow hall into the small room dimmed as the two men entered. The larger man who came first seemed to dwarf the room. He was dressed in an expensively cut business suit that somehow was coordinated perfectly with the mass of rusty colored whiskers tumbling onto his chest. His massive hands were immaculately manicured, and one could not help but notice the ring on his right hand. Its setting consisted of one diamond that could not have been less than two carats.

The man who followed, although large of his own accord, seemed small in comparison. In contrast to his companion, he was dressed in working clothes, snug jeans and a flannel shirt. His face was shadowed with a beat-up felt hat, but there was something about him that caught your attention: the double barreled shotgun in the crook of his arm.

"Well, well Mr. Stokes, I see Ruby has brought your dinner," the first man offered. "You mustn't think we're uncultured just because we've had a difference of opinion. Not only is the cuisine excellent, but I trust you'll fancy this evening's entertainment as well."

As the man spoke, Ruby's eyes darted furtively from face to face, and she began toying nervously with a loose strand of hair. She had seen Mr. Baxter's "entertainments" before, and while they always scared her, she was simultaneously attracted and repulsed. She remembered the last one vividly.

"Yes, Yes," Mr. Baxter continued, "I think we'll have a little game. Could I interest you, perhaps, in some Russian Roulette?"

Frank Stokes still slumped in his chair, but his eyes moved quickly to the shotgun.

"No, no, Mr. Stokes," the big man admonished, "not that kind of Russian Roulette, although I'm sure Jess would gladly oblige you. Actually, I had something a little more lively in mind."

So it was to be the snakes after all. Frank Stokes drew his breath in sharply. His adrenalin rushed as he recalled his first "game" with the snakes. He had been lucky that the snake had been cold and sluggish. Only a small amount of venom had entered his system. They said in these parts that if you didn't die from a rattlesnake bite you'd wished you had. They were right. He had been sick three months, and his stomach turned now at the thought of it.

"Now, Mr. Stokes, shall we begin?" Mr. Baxter inquired politely. "It's really very simple. All you have to do is take out one little snake and then put it back in. If fortune is on your side, you'll live to play another night. If not, well, I think you know more about that than the rest of us do."

Mr. Baxter signaled to Jess who lifted the heavy screen from the top of the giant aquarium. Then he reached in with the barrel of his shotgun and prodded the snakes. The game was ready.

A cold sweat broke out on Frank Stokes' face. He wished he were dead, but he knew there was no way out of this nightmare. Baxter had every intention of seeing this game through, and if he, Frank, didn't play along, Baxter wouldn't hesitate to play his trump card, Frank's 19 year old daughter, Laura. Frank Stokes cursed himself for being a fool. One round with the snakes should have convinced him that these people played for keeps, but his shame for his participation in their crimes, even though coerced, had goaded him into a second act of defiance, and now he had to take his medicine.

Slowly he rose from the beat up wooden table and approached the big aquarium of snakes. Whatever kind of fool he was, he wasn't a damn fool. He had seen some of the local men snatch up poisonous snakes by the tail and snap their heads off. He knew that his survival depended on split second timing and superb eye-hand coordination. But then wasn't that why he was here? Wasn't it that natural combination of steel-like nerves and steady, lightening quick hands that made him what he was, the best diamond cutter west of the Mississippi?

Frank concentrated steadily on the snakes as if they were precious stones, and the rest of the room disappeared. Gradually he slowed his breathing until the pounding in his temples subsided. Then in what seemed like an instant, he dipped into the aquarium and withdrew his arm. Clenched in his fist was one large, hideous snake. With obvious distaste, he released the snake and watched it drop back on top of the others. Only then did he become aware of the three other people still in the room.

"Very good, Mr. Stokes," Baxter began in his carefully modulated voice. "I see your timing hasn't suffered along with your conscience. Now, will it be back to work, or shall we continue our game tomorrow?" Stokes choked down the hatred swelling in his chest. He had been lucky tonight. Even the best snake hunters avoided a nest of riled snakes. His chances of survival a second night were at best questionable.

—w—

Later that evening, C. William, "Big Bill", Baxter sat behind the massive desk in the large office at the back of the old farm house up the hill from the earth house. There was a knock on the door and Jess entered.

"Did he give you any more trouble?" Baxter inquired.

"No," Jess responded. "I reckon that snake trick about took the wind out of his sails. He'll be easy to handle, for a while anyway. I still can't figure out how you knew he'd be able to pull that stunt off."

"Very simple," smiled Big Bill. "Necessity is the mother of invention, and all that esoteric rhetoric. But then you're quite right. If he hadn't 'pulled that stunt off', as you say, we'd be in a good bit of trouble. So, I took the precaution of loading the deck in my favor. Those snakes have been defanged. They can still strike, but they can't inject any venom. I figure the shock of the strike alone will serve our purposes nicely. But let's keep that our little secret shall we, in case Mr. Stokes should become troublesome again?"

Jess's mouth widened into a slow grin of approval, and he slapped his thigh in silent mirth. Big Bill was sure some thinker, he was."Now about our other little problem," Big Bill changed the subject. "What have you found"?

"Well now, the nearest I can figure," Jess responded, "she's eatin' them. I've been watchin' her real close on the close-circuit, and she's awful sneaky. She never touches any part of her body when she's in the diamond room except her mouth. You know how she kinda chews her fingernails? So I put a trap under her toilet, and sure 'nough it's all smushed up like somebody's been lookin' for somethin' darn small in it!"

"I see," said Baxter thoughtfully. He pressed his fingers together and rested his chin on his index fingers with his elbows on the desk, as if contemplating a deep problem. "That's too bad. It'll be quite inconvenient to replace Ruby, but I guess it can't be helped. You'd better bring up someone from the earth house to guard the girl, and we'll have to send someone besides you for supplies for a few days. You're sure she's not suspicious? Well, then we'd better do it tonight. I trust you know a convenient spot?"

Jess nodded his answer then quietly left the office.

—⚡—

Ruby was a chronic insomniac. She slouched in an old overstuffed chair in front of the T.V. watching a late night talk show. The reception back in the woods could only be described as awful, but that didn't deter the faithful Ruby. She leaned forward and increased the volume as the guest host continued his monologue on the finer points of shampooing a cat. As she watched, she absent-mindedly fondled the hem of her blue gingham dress. Big Bill was awful careful about the diamonds. When you went into the counting room, they watched you like a hawk. You had to strip off and put on a hospital-like gown with no pockets, no cuffs, no anything. Then they checked your hair when you came out. She had been very careful, only a single diamond here and there, but during the last year she'd built up a little nest egg, and nobody was the wiser. Even now, there were two nice little diamonds sewn securely into the hem of her dress. She kept them there until she had the chance to move them to her safe place. But she liked to keep her newest acquisitions with her just in case she had to leave in a hurry.

Ruby heard the door to the hall open, and Jess came in. "Boss wants to see you," he said.

Ruby sighed deeply as she tore herself away from the sexy hunk talking to the host. She'd never understand why some people had to wait 'til after midnight to conduct their business, but Big Bill had a habit of calling her at all hours of the night. She wondered if he ever slept.

Ruby moved down the hall toward the back of the house as Jess followed. She stopped in the kitchen and took a 6-pack of beer out of the refrigerator. Big Bill encouraged everyone to have a beer or two when they had these late night conferences. He'd probably have B&B himself, but the beer was a good-will symbol for his workers.

Big Bill looked up as Jess and Ruby entered the office. His smile belied the treachery in his mind. "Come in, Ruby, Jess," he invited. "I have something

I need to talk to you about. Do you remember my mentioning Operation Willowcreek?"

They both nodded, and he continued. "Well, it seems they've run into a little snag; they've had a woman come down with an appendicitis attack, and she had to be hospitalized. It seems that one of her charges is a cantankerous old lady who still thinks she's running the company. They'd like to keep it that way, so naturally they need someone immediately to fill in until their woman recovers. It shouldn't be more than a week or two at the most. With laparoscopy being so readily available, recovery time is almost negligible. Do you think you could do it, Ruby?"

"Well, yeah, I expect I could. But who'd take over for me here?" asked Ruby.

"That's why Jess is here," Big Bill responded smoothly. "Jess, do you think you can handle Ruby's end of it for a week or two? There will, of course, be a cash bonus for both of you. In advance." He opened the drawer in front of him and casually laid out two large piles of bills.

Ruby didn't dare ask how big the bonus was, but she could tell it was plenty. What luck! A vacation with a bonus. Getting out of these woods and away from that creepy earth house for a while suited her fine. "Well if Jess don't mind, I reckon I don't either. A little change of scenery is good for the soul, I always say," she responded.

Jess hunched his shoulders in acceptance.

"When do I leave?" asked Ruby.

"Could you be ready in about half an hour?" Big Bill queried. "You won't need much, just a suitcase. You know that we prefer that our people travel lightly. And, oh yes, Ruby, I'm sure Jess would appreciate your making a list of anything unusual he should watch for. I'll call the Willowcreek people while you're packing to find out a safe place to meet them. I'll be going along too since I have some personal business to attend to."

Ruby clutched her purse in her lap as she sat in the back of the old car. Two thousand dollars! She could hardly believe her good fortune. It was very late, or very early, whichever you preferred, and she dozed off now and then. They'd been driving back roads for about an hour now. They'd crossed from Pope into Faulkner County, and now they were winding around the hills back in the direction they had come from on a black snake of a road. The moon was full, and the clouds were clearing so you could see open pastures and dark barns. The car dipped down into a small valley and slowed to a stop at a narrow concrete bridge spanning a gurgling creek.

"OK," Jess said. "This is where we met last time. Everything looks clear to me."

"Very well, "Mr. Baxter agreed. "Let's give them the signal. Ruby, do you see that little dirt road at the end of the bridge? They'll be parked down there a short distance in view of the bridge. Now I want you to get out and stand up on that little concrete rail toward the middle. If everything is safe, they'll signal with their lights."

Ruby opened the back door of the car and climbed out. All this secret code stuff always seemed silly to her, but Big Bill knew what he was doing, and he'd never led her wrong yet. As she walked to the center of the bridge, she heard Jess get out behind her. Jess was probably going to take a whiz. Jess was always taking whizzes in the woods. Unlike Big Bill, the man had been raised in a barn. She climbed up awkwardly onto the 10 inch railing bordering the bridge. She could hear and smell the creek, which was swollen from the recent rain, passing beneath her. Just then she felt the probe of cold metal in her back, and somewhere, far away, she heard an explosion. The waters from the spring rains rushed up to meet her, and Ruby was no more.

About The Author

Beryl Wealand is a retired anatomy professor who lets her alter-ego, Dr. Garnet Daniels solve mysteries surrounding Arkansas River Valley events. Garnet is aided by her niece, Colleen, and numerous relatives and friends. The professionals and local characters in Beryl's books are drawn from memories created during many years of teaching and living in the Ozark Mountains.

www.ingramcontent.com/pod-product-compliance
Lightning Source LLC
Chambersburg PA
CBHW070549130626
46556CB00001B/86